Here We Go

Chloe Porter

Contents

CHAPTER ONE - Here We Go Again

Tyson POV

There was something seriously weird about this chick. And I don't mean the fact that she looked like she just got off the set of an action movie, although her clothes were definitely strange. No. What nagged me was the fact that she still wasn't afraid of me. I had a certain reputation in this town and even if a foreigner like her didn't know about it, she should have figured it out by now. But instead, when I caught her hand after she lashed out on me, all she did was look surprised. And now that I had countered her next few moves that look had turned into one of annoyance instead of what she should have felt: fear. But if she still didn't get it, then it was time to stop being a gentleman. With that thought in mind I took a swing at her face and it was my turn to be taken aback as she swiftly dodged it and her fist collided with my stomach.

Okay, now I was really angry!

*****

Alex POV

The boy I was fighting with was really, really good. And that means a lot coming from someone with my experience. How I got into this mess you ask?

Well, it all began with me moving into this shitty small town to start anew. To make a long story short, I got into some trouble back at home so my parents exiled me here. Which had its good sides considering who I left behind. But that's a whole different story.

The weather outside was warm tonight with a nice cool breeze, so I'd decided to take a walk. I'd put on my combat boots, long black leather pants, strapless short black top that only covered my breast area, fingerless leather gloves and a knee length light black coat that I kept unbuttoned. Yes, you've guessed it, black was my favorite color. I didn't have any jewelry on apart from the two things I always wore - the thick, engraved silver earring on the lowest hole of my right ear and my silver locket. Tonight it was hooked to a thick long chain and it reached my naked stomach.

I got outside of my apartment and not knowing the town that well yet, I headed for nowhere in particular. I was just turning round a corner when a street cat jumped in front of me. Startled to see me there, it froze. We stared at each other for a while before I nodded at it to move first. As if the cat understood me, it did. But before it disappeared from my vision it turned its head back and meowed.

"You're welcome!" I shouted after it. I didn't know why I did that; it wasn't like the animal could understand me word by word.

I heard someone's throaty laugh coming from behind me and turned to see who it was. After a few seconds of searching I found the source of the noise: a boy, who was leaning casually against one of the near-by buildings. He kept himself in the shadows so I had to squint my eyes slightly in an attempt to see him more clearly. He was medium height, seemingly about my age and had long dark hair that was tied in a low ponytail.

"Did you just speak to an animal?" His voice was musical even with the mocking inflection it held.

"And what if I did?" I asked jutting my chin up stubbornly.

"Then you're even weirder than I thought." He answered pushing himself off the wall and coming closer to me. He was only a step away from me when he finally stopped walking.

Now that he was standing under the streetlight, I looked at him again.

"Well built with practical casual clothing; right handed, definitely strong, probably fast too..." I silently listed in my mind. Then I sighed, realizing I was assessing whether he was a threat or not if we were to get into a strife. I guess old habits die hard!

I noticed he was checking me out, a sneering expression on his otherwise handsome face. That made me want to punch him straight in the jaw but luckily for him, I'd recently promised myself to try not to start fights.

Without taking his eyes off of me he reached into the back pocket of his dark blue jeans getting out a packet of cigarettes, taking one out and lighting it before returning the rest of his smokes to their original place. Being a habitual non-smoker, the cig's reek assaulted my nose and it automatically wrinkled.

He smirked at my reaction. Seriously? He dared to smirk at me? This boy really must have a death wish!

"Does this bother you?" He said, now rolling his smoke between his fingers.

"Yes! And I'm going to make sure you're bothered too, if you don't get it away from my face," I growled at him.

His arm froze in the air just as he was about to place the cig between his shapely lips again. The boy's eyes widened slightly and he looked at me with an unbelieving expression. Perhaps he wasn't used to people talking back at him or maybe he was just stunned that a girl of five feet was threatening him. I've often been depreciated because of my size, but let me tell you this: underestimate me and I'll make you pay for that dearly.

The boy's astonishment lasted only a moment. From surprised and unbelieving, his face quickly turned into amused and sneering again, and he barked another loud laugh. He then took one long drag from his cig before leaning down and slowly exhaling in my face.

That was it! That was the last straw!

I looked the boy dead in the eye and took a swing at his face.

*****

Tyson POV

We must have been fighting for almost ten minutes now. It usually took me a lot less to knock somebody down especially in a one on one but this chick was fucking fast! And experienced. Very experienced.

Her aim was good, she knew the right spots to hit or kick and she twisted around as if she didn't have a single bone in her body. Somehow I finally manage to kick her behind the knees, landing her on the ground. I quickly jumped on top of her, but before I could pin her down completely, she reversed our positions so that she was now above me. It was a basic move and I couldn't believe I actually fell for it. I was momentarily taken aback, but a second later I rolled us over so that I straddling her and attempted to pin her hands with mine. She glared furiously at me and started thrashing around, trying to get free.

As if I was going to let her!

We both froze when we heard them. The shrill sound of the police cars' sirens was getting louder and louder. I didn't know if someone had called to report our fight or was it just a coincidence, but either way, they were getting closer.

Taking one last look at the girl below me, I got up and ran away. If she was smart, she'd be doing the same.

*****

I got to my house at about four in the morning. I was tired from the fight and the running after we got interrupted by the sirens. I craved some rest but was covered in dirt from our not so little scuffle, so I went to take a shower first. Plus, I had some bruises to take care of. I'm pretty sure I left a few marks on her body as well.

I felt a pang of guilt at that thought; I've never hit a girl before. Never even imagined that one day I would.

I stood under the shower, hoping that the lukewarm water would help me clear my mind. But tonight's events stubbornly refused to leave my head.

Why did I start a fight with this chick? Technically, it was she who threw the first punch (or at least tried to), but perhaps I acted a bit as a jerk to her... Okay, I acted like a complete asshole, no perhaps about it.

First I laughed at her, then I called her weird... And why did I blow cigarette smoke in her face again?

It wasn't like me to act this way. My motto was "leave people alone, so you'll be left alone" and it suited me just fine. I didn't need or want anybody meddling in my private life and I could definitely take care of myself, so why bother making new acquaintances?

Getting out of the shower, I absentmindedly took care of my wounds. Since I often got into fights, I had everything needed stored on the rickety bathroom stand. I was on my way out when I glanced at the cracked mirror above the sink and stopped dead in my tracks.

I remembered the girl slapping my face at some point and me feeling a stinging sensation but I was so pissed off at that moment that I just ignored it. Anger boiled through me now. There, on my left cheek, stood four fresh nail marks. I didn't even realize I had them!

I'm going to murder that little bitch!

CHAPTER TWO - One very long Monday - PART ONE

- -

Tyson POV

I was running late for class again but that didn't make me speed up. I'd been working three nights in a row. My whole body was in bruises and I was so tired that I should've been given a medal for showing up at all. That's how I saw it anyway. Apparently, my homeroom teacher - Mr. Johnson, disagreed.

"How nice of you to finally join us!" Was the sarcastic greeting I got from him when I opened the classroom door.

Why did teachers always replay with something as prosaic as that whenever someone was late? I heard him giving me detention, but I didn't even bother to make up an excuse and try to get out of it. I just stalked to my seat in the back of the classroom. But before I reached my destination I saw that the one next to it (that was usually empty 'cause I scared anybody who attempted to sit there) was now taken by somebody new. Well, new for the class anyway, because I would recognize her anywhere. She kept her head down and her brown hair was covering her face but I knew it was her; I knew it was the girl I got in a fight with just a few nights ago. Hope she wouldn't cause a scene, I hated those. She glanced at me briefly when I sat down and I tried to read her eyes. Her stare was completely blank: there was no surprise, no glimmer of recognition, no anger, no fear.

How could she not recognize me?! Yes, we met only once and yes, it had been dark, but it wasn't that dark! If I saw her features clearly, then she must have seen mine. I mean we were practically face to face at some point. Besides, eyes like mine were hard to forget.

How come she did not remember me?

I frowned and looked through the window on my left. That was why I choose to sit here – so that I could stare through it. It was how I'd spent my time in this and many other classes. I would gaze out and watch whatever's happening there. It was usually more intriguing than what happened during lessons.

But today I couldn't help but sneak glances at the girl sitting to my right. She spent the whole time doodling in her very scruffy notebook not paying any attention to the teacher or anyone else. Not paying any attention to me. She was just sitting there drawing some complicated twisted designs and bobbing her head rhythmically. It took me a while to realize her long hair was hiding a set of headphones.

I wondered what she was listening to.

"Why should I care?" Was my next thought.

I looked at the clock that was located over the door. Great, ten more minutes! That's ten too many for my liking! I looked at the girl again. She had opened a new page and had started sketching a face. Not too bad I might add. It wasn't as good as her doodles but still...

Ugh! Why was I even paying attention to the little bitch?

The bell finally rang and I was just about to get up when I saw the girl hadn't moved. Maybe she didn't hear it because she was listening to music. I saw that some of our classmates had already left but I decided to stall and pretended to be tying my shoe. I know, lame excuse, but it worked.

I heard the door close shut and realized that the two of us were the only ones left in the room. Suddenly the girl jumped from her seat and tried to grab me by the throat. Tried being the key word here because I caught her arm.

"Huh, she went for the throat again." I thought and felt a smirk forming on my lips.

"What the fuck are you doing here?" She spat angrily at my face. I guess she remembered me after all. For some reason that made my smirk even wider.

"I study here." I answered calmly, knowing that tone would work her up.

"You don't seem like the studying type to me." She growled and tried to hit me with her free hand. I caught that one as well.

"Let. Me. Go." She commanded with her tone dangerously low.

"Maybe I don't want to."

At that she tried to kick me but I managed to avoid it. We heard voices outside the room and her head turned to the door.

"Shit!" The girl muttered. "Okay, let me go! I won't hit you... for now." She muttered the last part.

"Are you afraid that someone might see us fighting?"

"You should be the one worried about getting caught abusing a girl." The brunette turned to me with a slight smirk.

"I know what you are doing and it's not going to work on me, short stuff! I'm not letting you go until you admit what we both know: I'm better than you. And If we hadn't been interrupted that night, I would've won."

"Then we're going to be here for a long, long time, 'cause I'm pretty sure I could've kicked your ass." She looked at me defiantly, thrusting her chin forward in the very same manner she did when we first met.

I was just about to reply that I was in no hurry when somebody's enraged tone came from the direction of the door.

"Mr. Williams let go of Miss Atanasova this instance!"

The angry and perhaps slightly panicked voice belonged to our homeroom teacher. I looked at "Miss Atanasova" to see her smirking. Oh, she got just what she wanted: me taking the blame for this. Then again, if I was Johnson and walked into my classroom to see the notorious Tyson Williams man-handling the small, deceptively defenseless new girl, I'd be worried too.

I held her gaze for a moment and let her go. Before I walked away though I whispered that we were going to finish this later. Her smirk only widened and just as quietly she responded with "I'm looking forward to it".

*****

Alexandra. That was her first name. I found it out when she introduced herself to my second period teacher: a considerably plump, short man in his late forties.

Apparently English was another class we had together. The teacher told her to take a seat and she headed straight to the back of the classroom. This time it was her who sat down next to me, surely for the sole purpose of pissing me off.

I took in her features: fair complexion; long brown hair that was dark at the roots but became lighter at the ends, which were forming soft but messy waves; big round brown eyes; small pale pink lips; a round mouth kept slightly ajar. She wasn't wearing layers of makeup like most girls from our school, just a thin line of eyeliner on her lower eyelid. Her clothes were far more casual than last time we met: grey singlet, that showed off her toned arms, black jeans and black sneakers. Her short black leather jacket was spread on the back of her chair. She wore the same locket as last time only it was now attached to a leather choker, its design matching that of the leather cuff-like bracelets that were circling her wrists. There were two bright red dots piercing her left ear and two black ones on her right along with a thick silver earring.

"No matter how long you stare, you won't intimidate me." She said quietly so that only I could hear her. She didn't even bother to look my way, probably observing me with her peripheral vision. Or maybe she had just felt my gaze on her.

"No matter how tough you try to act, I'm still stronger than you." I kept my voice down as well when I replied.

The girl turned her head towards me and I saw anger flash in those chocolate brown orbs of hers. She quickly got a hold on herself and adopted a smug expression.

"Physically stronger, yes. But I'm flexible and agile. I'm not an easy target!"

"Funny, that's not how I remember it." I replied coolly.

"I landed you on your ass, didn't I?" She growled, leaning slightly towards me.

"Once."

"Twice." She corrected in that annoyingly smug tone of hers.

"No, it was only once." I was starting to get more and more annoyed by her behavior.

"No, it was twice. The second time was when you were on top of me but I managed to switch our places."

We heard someone clear their throat meaningfully. Both our heads snapped in the direction of the sound and we realized it came from our English teacher. He was staring at us with a peeved expression, but did not voice his irritation out loud. Some of our classmates were also looking at us with curious and slightly worried faces.

I didn't want to cause a scene and that was where we were headed, so I leaned back in my seat. The girl probably came to the same conclusion, because she followed suit. The teacher's features visibly relaxed and he went on with the lesson. Our classmates turned their heads to the whiteboard but I noticed they snuck glances towards Alexandra and I.

I gazed through the window in an attempt to calm myself. That didn't help and still feeling twitchy, I started tapping with my foot. A similar sound came from my right and when I turned, I saw the foreign girl was tapping her notebook with her pen.

My chair screeched as I leaned towards her and glared in her direction.

"That doesn't count!" She turned to me with a slightly confused expression, so I went on to clarify: "Switching our positions doesn't count as landing me on my ass!"

"Yes, it does!" She hissed, bringing her face closer to mine.

"No, it doesn't!" I snarled, leaning even more in her direction. By now our faces were only inches apart and our eyes, which were on the same level, burned with irritation.

"Mr. Williams, Miss Atanasova, is there something you would like to share with the class?" Our second period teacher asked.

"Nope." Alex popped the "p".

"Not really." Was my simultaneous answer.

"Than I suggest you keep quiet." The teacher reprimanded in a haughty tone.

"Just go on with your damn lesson already!" Alexandra replied annoyed.

Mr. Humpbag's face formed a surprised expression, before he replaced it with an angry grimace.

"Miss Atanasova, detention today after classes!"

"Whatever!" She waved her hand dismissively at him.

He just gapped at her dumbfounded.

"I don't know how things were at your previous school," he said trying to keep his voice even, "but here such behavior is not tolerated!"

"It wasn't tolerated there as well but that never stopped me before. Stop sweating it and go on with your lesson, Mr. Backhumper!"

"Humpbag!" He correcting her whilst shouting, no longer able to keep his cool.

"Backhumper sounds better to me." I mumbled but he must've heard me because he turned to face me.

"You two... OUT! NOW! Get out of my class! I don't want to hear any excuses!"

"Why would I give you an excuse to stick around?" I asked getting up.

"It's not like your class is making my day!" Alex added, following behind me and shutting the door, cutting off the sound of the animated whispers coming from our classmates. Once we were out of the classroom she turned to me.

"I believe you and I have something to finish."

"Want to do it here or in the courtyard?" I asked.

"Out. I don't want to be interrupted again."

I nodded and led her out to the back of the school. Everyone was in class so the only person we ran into in the hallway was the elderly janitor. He stopped his mopping to look us over and shake his disapprovingly before returning to his work. Once we got to the courtyard, we were on our own.

"You sure you want to do this?" I questioned her. She was irritating as hell but she was still a girl and a part of me (no matter how small in her case) was still rebelling against the thought of hitting her.

"Getting cold feet?" She asked smugly.

And that was all it took to fire me up. That tone, the sneering expression and the challenge in her eyes was something I could not resist.

"Shut up, bitch!" Was all I said before swinging at her with my right arm.

Alex used the same move as before blocking with her left and hitting me in the stomach with her right, effectively knocking the air out of me. I unconsciously took a step back, clutching the wounded place. She looked at me with narrowed eyes.

"I didn't hit you that hard." She muttered more to herself and took a few steps back before giving me the once-over. "Take off your shirt." She ordered in an even tone.

"Why?" I snarled at her but I already had a pretty good guess about her answer.

"Because I think you are injured and if that is the case I'm not fighting you 'till you get better. I don't want you to use it as an excuse when I kick your ass."

"I'm well enough to fight you. And you're not going to kick my ass."

"We'll see. Show me!"

Seeing the determination in her eyes, I reluctantly took off my top and waited for her reaction. I didn't expect her to panic when she saw my bruises; something was telling me this girl was used to such a sight.

"Someone sure did a number on you!" She whistled quietly.

"I fell down the stairs."

"Stairs... Yeah, it happens to me all the time... But you should see the state the stairs are in afterwards!" She gave me a small yet smug smile and turned to leave.

"Where do you think you're going?" I grabbed her by the arm. She cast me an even gaze and responded calmly:

"I decided not to fight you now. Call me when you're better!"

"I'm fine!" I hissed leaning my face to hers. She didn't look fazed at all. Did she have no self-defense instincts at all? I was obviously pissed at her, I was obviously stronger than her, and she just stood there completely unabashed. What the hell was wrong with this chick?

"Look, I already said I won't fight you. Even if you hit me I won't hit back."

"Then I'll just beat you up." I lied, hoping to make the girl reconsider. But the way she had replied with such determination in her chocolate brown eyes, made me realize she actually meant what she'd said.

"No, you won't. If I'm not hitting back, you'll lose interest," she called me on my bluff but I wasn't ready to give up just yet.

"What makes you say that?" I asked, giving her one of the most challenging glares I could muster.

"Because, as much as it pains me to say this, you and I have something in common. We both don't take shit from nobody, we both enjoy teaching whoever stands in out way a lesson and we both like a fair fight. That's how I know you'll lose interest if I don't respond, because that's what I would do if our roles were switched."

At that she wrenched her wrist from my hand and left. I didn't even try to stop her this time, because although I didn't want to admit it, I knew she was right.

CHAPTER THREE -
One very long Monday -
PART TWO

A lex POV

"So this was the infamous Tyson Williams that I've heard about," I thought while walking back inside the school.

It seemed that the rumors were true. I knew people that were in the same line of... business as him and I had heard a lot about his personality. He was unpredictable, never backing down and with a short fuse; but those were only to his benefit with what he did for a living. Or maybe that was a side deal for him and he only got into fights to vent off some frustration. Either way I was glad that I didn't almost get my ass kicked by some random guy. How didn't I figure out who he was sooner though? Maybe because I hadn't heard anything about his appearance. Then again I knew these things about him from guys. I bet if a girl was describing him she would've definitely talked about his looks. And boy, would she have something to talk about!

The boy was gorgeous. I wouldn't usually use this word for a guy, but that was the best way to describe him. He was about five feet ten and with one hell of a body: pure muscle everywhere. And I don't mean the ridiculous body-builder type with wide shoulders and itsy-bitsy waist. No, just good old-fashioned proportional masculine body. His skin was a pale, but healthy shade. His hair was black and long, passing his shoulders and some of it fell into his eyes. He had a handsome face with defined features and a strong jaw line. Even the slightly crooked nose, probably broken at some point thanks to his lifestyle, did little to reduce the boy's fine looks. He had nicely shaped soft-looking lips. But the most amazing thing about him was his eyes; his mismatched eyes. One bright blue orb and one silvery-grey. Not only were they differently tinted, but the shades of those two colors were pretty unique by themselves. Add that up to all the strength illuminating those eyes and he could easily hypnotize people with them.

Well, they definitely got me distracted just thinking about them; I didn't even hear the bell ring but the hallways were full of people now. I turned round a corner and something bumped into me. Something that squealed and poured its drink over my jacket.

"I am so, so very sorry!" The girl started to apologize looking at my now wet clothing. "I didn't..." She trailed off finally noticing who I was. I remembered her from second period and because of my little disagreement with that teacher she probably thought I was going to snap at her. So what I did was put on my friendly face and say in the most gentle voice I could muster at the moment:

"It's okay. It's not like you did it on purpose so don't worry about it." And I really meant it.

She looked at me doubtingly, then glanced at her group of friends that were behind her. I noticed one of the boys, the one with sandy blond hair and tanned skin, look especially tense. His eyes were darting from me to the little (although still taller than me) redhead and then back again. He was obviously worried that I would hurt her. Hmm, maybe the boy had a crush on her. They would make a cute couple, both seemed really decent. Actually, their whole group appeared to be so. I smiled to myself. I didn't hit people like that. If I were to do it, I would feel terribly guilty about it afterwards.

"As I already said," I turned to the redhead once more, trying to calm her down, "it was an accident. But if you are feeling guilty about it you could show me where the restrooms are 'cause I have no fucking clue."

"Okay…" She trailed off, but I could see she was still worried. Damn, why did I have to snap at the teacher? Way to keep a low profile, Alex!

"I'll come too." Mr. Sandy Blond said with a slight Australian accent and placed himself between me and the girl. Yep, he definitely liked her.

"I'm Alexandra by the way."

"I'm Tara and this is Danny." The redhead responded, separating from her little posse with me and Blondie in tow. As we walked I noticed several people smiling and waving at her, then freezing as they noticed me. The moment I had passed them, I could hear them whispering behind my back. Well, I guess I was starting to gain some popularity.

"Lucky me!" I thought sardonically.

"So what year are you guys?" I already knew about the girl but decided to make some small talk nonetheless. It wasn't really my thing, but she still seemed a bit uneasy and I hoped that would help her and the boy relax.

"We're both seniors." Tara answered opening the door to the girls' bathroom and going in with me. I noticed Danny wasn't happy about having to wait outside as he glared at me and groaned quietly in irritation. I made sure to aim a smirk his way before I closed the door.

Going to one of the sinks, I took off my jacket and started washing off the stain. Two girls, who were applying even more makeup to their already generously painted faces, looked me over and rolled their eyes. I decide to give them the cold shoulder; such empty-headed bimbos were not worth my time anyway. I worked in silence, trying my best to ignore them gushing about some jock called Mike Barbson, who apparently had "looks to die for" and was throwing a party this Friday. The girls finally left, squealing about how they "so have to shop for the party" and buy "something to make the guys fight over" them. I snorted at that. What kind of idiots would get in a tussle for someone as cheap as these two seemed to be?

I turned on the hand drier and held my clothing under it.

"So..." Tara trailed off.

"You thought I would snap at you, didn't you?" I asked her, moving my gaze from the jacket and onto her face.

"Pretty much." She admitted shyly.

I laughed.

"Do I look that scary?"

"No." She smiled herself. "But I was in the room when you got into your argument with Mr. Humpbag."

"So you thought I would be like that towards everyone?" She nodded. "Look, Tara, I just didn't like the dude. He's a bloody lame teacher. Plus he's pushy and demanding and I don't fucking follow orders."

"Do you always cuss this much?"

"I'm Bulgarian; it's in my blood." I explained giving her a wink. She laughed. "Do you still think I'm going to punch you?"

"Nope."

"Good! 'Cause I'm not. I don't like hitting people who can't defend themselves and no offense, but you don't strike me as a warrior."

"Nah, I'm pretty clumsy." She admitted cheerfully, all signs of her previous distress gone. "So what do you have now?"

I reached into the back pocket of my black jeans and took out the sheet with my schedule. This was my first day and the piece of paper had already crumpled. I glanced at it and groaned.

"Math."

For some reason that made the other girl smile.

"So do I. Come on, I'll show you where it is."

*****

I was sitting too close to the whiteboard for my liking. But Tara, being the good girl she was, preferred placing her ass at the front. And I, trying to be nice to her, sat there as well because no one else from her group shared this class with us. I liked sitting in the back, further away from the teachers. Plus that way I was sheltered from the curious looks of my classmates. And from the less-than-friendly gaze of one particular set of mismatched eyes. Yes, ladies and gentlemen, Tyson Williams and I shared yet another class. Only this time he had a strategic advantage because I couldn't see him since he was once more at the back. I could feel him staring at my nape. God, I wanted to spring out of my chair and punch him! Now that I knew who he was, he presented an even bigger challenge. And I don't back down on challenges. But no, I had to stay put. After all I moved to this God-forsaken town to start anew. I really shouldn't be getting into unnecessary fights. I should try to be a good girl: less rows, less parties, less trouble… sadly that meant less fun. But how was I to do that when Tyson was here? Just the thought of him made my blood boil. It's been quite a while since somebody had the upper hand against me in a one on one. Except for him of course. But I really shouldn't be remembering him if I wanted to calm down. Come to think of it he and the boy currently sitting at the back of the class were somehow similar. Oh, great! I moved away from that guy only to end up in the same town and school with a boy just like him!

*****

Tyson POV

I wanted to fight her. So what if I was injured? To hell with that! I wanted to show her I wasn't somebody she could push around and I couldn't wait to do so. Patience had never been amongst my virtues. I thought that if I see her in third period I would convince her to fight me. I bet that won't be difficult; she appeared to be just as short-tempered as I was, so maybe I could piss her off enough for her to ignore my wounds. I mean, she managed to peeve me enough to overlook the fact that she was a girl and get into a tussle with her. And if I didn't catch her during Math there was always lunch. I could just pull her into an empty room and "politely" explain how things are run around here… I was at the top of the food chain. I just had to wait until no one was around. It would be easy to do so because she looked like a loner. But no! She decided to make some new friends and join one of the herds around here. Yes, the social groups were pretty much like herds: one leads, the others follow.

So now Alex was eating lunch and laughing with about ten other people all of whom seemed completely charmed by her. All but a sandy blond-haired boy who was looking at her with suspicion clear in his gaze and a dark-haired girl who was glaring in the foreigner's direction, probably jealous because she wasn't the center of attention. I noticed that the redhead Alex sat next to during Math was also there.

How was I to get her alone now? Maybe I should wait until school ends. I could get out of the last class early and wait for her at the gates. If she was with somebody, I could stalk her until they separated and then…

WHAT THE HELL WAS I THINKING?! Stalking? Fucking stalking her?! What the fuck was she doing to me? I wasn't that type of person. She made me think so irrational. Dumb bitch. Now I wanted to hit her even more than before!

*****

Lessons had ended and I was dragging my feet in the now empty hallway, heading for detention. Our school penal system was such that the teachers were on a rotating schedule, so I didn't know who I would get to supervise me today. Sometimes I would get a teacher I didn't even have classes with.

Just as I was about to turn the corner something small bumped into me. I let out a loud "Ugh!" simultaneously with the other person's "Ouch!" I looked down to none other than my newest personal nightmare.

"Watch where you're going!" Alex gave me a dirty look.

"You were the one running around, not paying attention." I glared back.

"If you saw that I was distracted why didn't you step aside?" She shot back.

"I don't make way for anybody."

"You might want to change that around me!" She hissed threateningly.

I lowered myself so our faces were on the same level.

"Listen and listen well! I rule around here. I might've gone easy on you the first time 'cause you're a girl but if you keep pissing me off, I won't be so gentle next time."

"Good! I like it rough!" She smirked mockingly.

"I'm not kidding, shorty! You better cut it out!"

"I would usually say "make me" but then I would have to punch you and I hate hitting the sick and injured."

With that she turned to leave but I pushed her violently so that her back hit the lockers. I placed my hands on either side of her head, trapping her between the metallic lockers and my body. The girl didn't even flinch. No, she actually seemed amused and the smirk was back on her lips.

"You know..." Alex started with a playful tone, "if someone sees us like this they might get a totally wrong impression about our... relationship."

I grunted, knowing exactly what she was implying to.

"As if I would make out with a bitch like you!"

She opened her mouth to speak but was cut off by the sound of approaching footsteps. Reluctantly, I pushed myself away from her just as one of our teachers approached.

"Aren't you two supposed to be in detention?" Mr. Johnson reprimanded.

"We were just getting there." Alex replied. I had forgotten Humpbag made her stay after classes.

"Then what are you doing still in the hallway?" Johnson asked impatiently.

"We were having a discussion about the social statuses around here." She answered with a smile that didn't reach her eyes and we both turned away from the guy and headed for our hour of redemption.

*****

Alex POV

I was on my way to detention with Tyson by my side. I wasn't going to let him out of my sight. I didn't trust the boy and thought he might attack me from the back. He probably came to the same conclusion about me because he kept sneaking suspicious glances my way.

"You're late!" A very irritated voice bellowed at us the moment we opened the door to the classroom where detention was held.

"Sorry, Mr. Backhumper!" I said to the plump man.

"Humpbag!" He growled at me.

I looked around the room. It seemed like your regular classroom with paled from time walls, old desks and chairs made from wood and metal, and a small whiteboard. There was only one more person here beside the teacher. Tyson's features softened almost insensibly at the sight of the other student and he headed in his direction. The boy looked up from his notebook and smiled at the newcomer. Tyson gave him a quick nod in response and sat down to his left. I followed him and sat to the boy's right. I discretely checked out the unfamiliar face.

The boy looked good. He was medium height, fit and slightly muscled. He had short spiky brown hair and kind blue eyes. The features of his face were soft and gave off the impression of an amiable person. I noticed he was sneaking peeks at me so I gave him a smile. He returned it immediately.

Tyson shifted in his seat before saying:

"No need to be polite to her, Angel; she's a real bitch."

"Quiet!" Mr. Humpbag shouted just as the door opened and a strict looking woman entered the room.

"Mr. Humpbag," she started with an annoyingly snobbish voice, "a word, if you please?"

"Stay here and keep quiet!" The male teacher snarled at us before both of them left the room. As soon as the door closed behind them, I turned to the cutie at my left with a friendly smile.

"Hi, Angel! I'm Alex." I introduced myself, extending my hand in greeting.

"Hello, Alex!" He said shaking it.

"Stay away from him, hoe!" Tyson growled making me smirk. He must be worried that I would lash out on his friend. My smile became even wider. Guess I found a new way to piss him off.

*****

Tyson POV

"What's the matter with you, Ty?" My childhood friend asked, turning to face me "She's just being friendly."

I snorted.

"Angel, that's the girl I've been telling you about."

"Huh?" He still wasn't getting it.

"The one from last week." I pointed at my left cheek where there still were faint marks. Being my only real friend, he was the sole person to whom I explained how I got them. Realization dawned on his features and he turned to look at Alex again.

"Wow!" He said with unadulterated admiration in his voice. He checked her out once again, this time more thoroughly. "Man, I wish I'd been there!" He admitted.

"Some best friend!" I thought bitterly.

Alex giggled.

"It was amusing." She said, winking at him.

"Oh, I bet it was! Do you know how many people can fight him one on one for so long and leave him with that many bruises? I'm pretty sure I can count them on the fingers of my hands."

"Shut up, Angel!" I snarled at him. Why did he have to tell her that?

"Come on, Ty! It won't kill you to admit she's good."

"Well, it's not true." I persisted. The truth was I didn't need her to know I thought she was good. Hell, I didn't even want to admit it to myself!

I heard my friend sigh in defeat before turning away from me.

"So, Alex, where are you from?" He asked politely. Why did he have to be so nice to people?

The two of us had met when we were children and we quickly took a liking to each other. But we were very different. I distanced myself from everyone and he was open and friendly; I tended glare and growl at people as means of communication and he was always polite; I had a short fuse and he was calm and reflective; the list went on. I guess our differences were what balanced us out and made us so close.

"Bulgaria." Alex's voice brought me to the present. "Heard of it?"

"Isn't it next to Greece?"

"Mhm. I got to admit I'm surprised you know it."

"I got to admit: I only checked it because of the Harry Potter series; geography isn't really my strong side." He laughed.

"Didn't I tell you to keep quiet?" Humpbag questioned, coming back into the room.

"You might've mentioned it, Mr. Backhumper." Alex replayed matter-of-factly. I've figured by now that she was purposefully misspelling his name in order to piss him off. Who could blame her? The dude was fucking annoying.

"My name is Humpbag, Miss Atanasova!" He growled at her, his face reddening.

"And mine is pronounced "A-ta-na-sova", not "A-te-ne-sova"!" She corrected coolly.

"Do not use that tone with me, missy!" Humpbag's face was getting redder by the minute. "I'm your teacher. Have some respect!"

"Respect and trust are two things to be earned. They are not given simply because of a title or position." She shot back irritated and I silently agreed. By the look on Angel's face, so did he. By the look on the teacher's face, those words only pissed him off more.

"You... I..." He seemed at a loss of words. "Get out! Now!"

"You're kicking me out of detention?" She asked wide-eyed and I was sure I looked the same.

"OUT! NOW!" He shouted heatedly, spit coming out of his mouth and falling on the floor and the front desks. Good thing we sat at the back!

"Okay, okay! I'm outing! I'm outing!" She said standing up. "Keep your wig on!" She added, exiting the premises.

Both Angel and I burst out laughing seeing Humpbag reach up to touch his fake hair with a look of pure horror on his face.

CHAPTER FOUR - Welcome to the posse

- -

A /N: Dedicated to @NickUskoski for helping me out so fast. That was awesome!

Important: He doesn't accept review/read requests so don't ask him.

*****

Alex POV

"Allie!" I heard Tara calling me. Her group had taken to addressing me like that because, just like my parents, they thought "Alex" was too masculine and, like one of the guys from the posse said, "not suitable for someone so cute". I never actually thought of myself as "cute" but oh, well...

"Hey, girl! What's up?"

"Nothing new." She shrugged then her smile fell from her freckled face. "How was detention?" She questioned dubiously.

"Interesting," I replied with a smirk. She answered me with a confused look, but before I could explain more, I heard Humpbag mispronouncing my name again.

"Ms. Atanasova! Detention!"

"Why? I just got here! I haven't done anything..."

"Yet," I added in my mind.

"Because of your behavior yesterday after classes. That is why: detention!"

I opened my mouth to protest, but then an idea came to my mind so I abandoned my initial tactic and went for another course of action.

"Well, if you want to spend more extracurricular time with me that badly..." I trailed off smiling impishly. I saw the teacher's face pale before he cleared his throat.

"As I was saying before you interrupted me," he began although we both knew I hadn't cut him off, "detention... is to be given to you if such behavior continues." He finished, turning on his heal and heading for his classroom.

"What was all that about?" Tara asked and led the way to our lockers. We were happy to find out that they were close to each other.

"I pissed him off yesterday, so he kicked me out of detention." I filled her in briefly.

"You got kicked out of detention yesterday?! And today you threatened your way out of one?"

I just shrugged nonchalantly, looking around, searching for one person in particular. But instead of him, I found his cute best friend rummaging through his locker.

"Hey, Angel!" I greeted and the boy answered me with a friendly smile.

"Hi, Alex! Got to warn you: Humpbag is looking for you and he seems furious."

"Yeah, I already saw him."

"Oh!" He exclaimed, no doubt taken aback by my unperturbed demeanor. "Did you get another detention?"

"Nope."

"How did you arrange that?"

"I asked nicely." I gave him a playful wink and left with Tara on my trail.

"You seem to be getting pretty popular." She remarked.

"You mean Angel? He's a nice guy."

"I know. But the people he hangs around with... Take Tyson Williams for example."

"Oh, I'll take him on as soon as he gets better!" I thought, while still listening to the redhead who walked beside me.

"That boy is trouble," she was just explaining. "He sometimes skips school for days and when he comes back he often has bruises or he's limping. The teachers tried to find out what was going on, but he never told them. Angel is the only person he actually talks to..."

"Morning, Tara!" Danny saluted, studiedly ignoring me.

"Hey, Danny!" Tara greeted back with a huge smile, immediately forgetting she had been telling me something. Oh, boy!

"Yeah... Hey, Danny." I saluted mockingly. "Walk with me!"

With that I pulled the boy by the wrist and dragged him away from our friend. I noticed the surprised and confused stares coming from the other students, but I didn't pay any attention to them and kept steering Dan in the direction I wanted. I found an empty room and pushed him in it, closing the door behind us with a little bit more force than I should have. Throughout our little walk, the boy hadn't uttered a single word or made any attempts to free himself, probably too stunned by my actions. Now that we were no longer moving, Danny got a hold of himself and frowning at me, he opened his mouth to talk.

"I'm not going to beat around the bush here." I spoke first, not giving him a chance to beat me to it. "I'm not going to hit her. I like Tara and she likes me. That means that we're going to spend a lot of time together. So you better deal with it and stop giving me attitude." I gave him a serious look. "I repeat: I don't want to hurt her!"

The boy stared at me with what I could only assume was supposed to be an intimidating expression, but he quickly gave up on the act and groaned in defeat.

"I know; I've noticed you aren't as bad as I originally thought." He reluctantly admitted in that cute Australian accent of his. "I'm just really worried about her. Our families are friends so we've known each other since we were kids and she's very... Umm... dear to me." I tried to hold back a smirk as I saw his cheeks redden slightly at that confession. Danny looked away in an attempt to compose himself and when he turned his face back to me, I saw his blue eyes shining with determination. "And if you ever do hurt her, I'm going to hit you regardless of you being a girl, Allie." He said firmly.

"Deal!" I chuckled shaking his hand. I decided not to tell him that I was capable of knocking him out with a single, well-aimed punch. He just seemed so resolved to protect Tara, it made me all soft and mushy inside. "Now let's get to our classes!"

*****

"He's not here either," I thought looking around the cafeteria. It seemed Tyson had resolved to skipping school today.

I sighed in irritation. I wanted to see how he was and maybe get into a few little refreshing quarrels with the boy just to keep him peeved till he was well enough to finish our fight. I knew that I'd promised myself to avoid exactly that type of behavior, but I couldn't help myself; that boy was so provoking that I was really looking forward to the challenge he presented. Not that having lunch with Tara and Danny's friends wasn't pleasant; most of them were really nice and they seemed to have taken a liking to me.

Except for Gloriana.

Glory, as the group called her, was in my humble opinion, an attention-seeking whore. And since I was the new girl, she saw me as a threat. She was constantly glaring at me and even dared to patronize me just so she could annoy me. I could easily fix that little problem, but she fell into the category of what I called "civilians". With that term I described anyone who wasn't brought up like me: raised to fight and prove their point with their fists. So no matter how much I wanted to beat the crap out of her, the best I could do was bitch slap her. But that would cause too much tension in our group so I settled to ignore her to the best of my extent. I couldn't help letting out some snappy comments every now and then though. I wouldn't be myself if I didn't.

I watched as a boy walked by our table, his eyes falling on Glory. I had to admit: her personality sucked, but the girl was a looker. She was about five feet seven, slender and with huge tits. Her long black hair was styled and not a single strand fell in her beautiful face. I thought about my untamed mane; I overslept this morning and didn't even bother to brush it, but even on a good day it still did as it pleased regardless of what I tried to do with it... But let's get back to Glory, shall we? She had tanned skin, green eyes and succulent lips. And she had on A LOT of makeup. But she pulled it off nicely and it looked stylish on her.

Probably noticing my intense gaze, the girl turned, narrowing her eyes in a nasty glare aimed at me.

Oops! Busted.

"Hey, Allie," Bella, a nice but extremely loud girl from our group addressed me and I turned towards her, "that is a beautiful locket." She reached to touch the round silver piece of jewelry, I always had on me. "Does it open?"

"No, it's jammed." I swiftly lied, without even batting an eye. I really didn't want to open it; what the silver roundel contained was just too private to show to complete strangers... or even someone I was close to. There were only two people, besides me, who knew what I had hid inside it and I had no intention on changing that number.

"Oh, Gosh, too bad!" She went on with her chatter, looking me over. "You have so many good-looking things... The locket and also the corset-like top you're wearing. It fits you perfectly! I wish I had that body!"

"You wish you had my body?" I repeated, deciding to tease her a bit. "Is that as in you wish you had a body like mine or do you want to make my body yours and do something naughty with me?"

She stared at me wide-eyed (as were the rest of the posse) and only managed to mutter: "I-I... Erm...". Ha! At last, Bella was speechless! It was a pleasant change as her constant gabble was getting on my nerves.

"Just kidding," I announced, stretching my arms lazily. "I know you just wish you had my body type."

"Oh, my Gosh, you had me there!" She said laughing out loud and most of the people at our table did the same.

"She sure had you, Bells!" Joey piped up from her left, giving the girl a playful nudge.

"Oh, yeah? You should've seen your face when you heard that, Joey!" Bella protested, smacking him on the shoulder and rolling her brown eyes when the boy let out an exaggerated cry of pain, making us laugh again.

"It wasn't even funny!" Glory growled through clenched teeth and got up to leave. A few girls literally jumped up from their seats in their haste to follow her, but all it took was for Glory to bark out "Stay!" without even sparing them a glance, and the girls immediately went back to their previous positions.

I followed her with my gaze, mildly aware that one of the cheerleaders - Trish, was talking about having an unofficial dance competition with some cheerleaders from another school.

"We were thinking about getting some sort of costumes for the dance off," she chirped enthusiastically. "Maybe a sexy army uniform or a police costume."

"Can't help you with the police uniform, but I have a cop-like hat that you could borrow as well as several pairs of handcuffs." I intervened, turning my head in her direction. I once again had everybody's full attention.

"Why do you have so many pairs of handcuffs?"

"You try to spread a person across your bed with just one pair!" I challenged and went back to eating the pizza I'd bought for lunch. I'd barely managed a bite when I heard all of them laugh again.

What was with that? Did they think I was kidding? 'Cause I sure as hell wasn't! I liked to spice things up and dressing up or blindfolding someone was definitely my kind of kink.

"It wasn't a joke." My statement wiped away their smiles and replaced them with stunned expressions. Some of them actually had their mouths gaping wide open in shock. "I'm a young girl, who has a clear view on her own limits and is not afraid to experiment or indulge herself in some grow-up activities. I really do have several pairs of handcuffs and I really have used them to tie someone to my bed; and FYI, they didn't mind at all."

A somewhat uncomfortable silence took place on our table. It was broken only by a few nervous throat clearings and the sound of cutlery being used. The other people in the cafeteria seemed oblivious as they kept on chatting, laughing, screaming and squealing their little hearts out. My female table-mates were attempting to avoid gazing at me, but I noticed some of the boys were looking me over with a renewed interest. Obviously I'd just earned myself the title of the kinkiest in the group and they were probably wondering whether I would be willing to give them a hands-on demonstration of how to use handcuffs the pleasurable way; without being shoved in a police car later. Because trust me, a uniformed man shoving you into a car to drive you to the nearest precinct is not a fun experience! Been there, done that. Not fun at all!

"So, Allie..." Danny started but he made a pause. What did he want to say? Or had he spoken out just to clear the air? "What was your previous school like?"

Well, that was a spur of the moment question if I've ever heard one!

"Yeah, what was it like?" Tara repeated with way too much enthusiasm. Yep. They were obviously trying to change the subject. I smiled inwardly at that; the two of them were so sweet!

"Which one?" I asked through a mouthful of pizza. "I've been to quite a few."

"How about the last one?" Joey helpfully proposed. He seemed to have gotten over his initial surprise about my naughty preferences.

"Yes, tell us about that!" Bella piped in as well.

"It was just a school; nothing special 'bout it." I shrugged. "Pretty much the same as here only smaller, grubbier and with even more annoying teachers." A few skeptical snorts followed my words and Joey muttered "There can be more annoying than what we have?"

"Actually, there is something in this school that I haven't encountered before: you."

"Us?" Tara asked in need of a clarification.

"Yes, you. All of you." I waved my hand around. "At this table, we have several cheerleaders, sitting next to a jock," I started to explain pointing at Trish, a few other girls and Joey, "and that is normal. But you guys also sit with Tara and Danny – the nice, quiet kids…"

"Who are you calling a kid? We're the same age!" Dan protested, his accent more prominent as he was obviously annoyed, but I ignored him and went on.

"They are quite popular, so I somewhat get that. Then there are the two Bellas – Isabella, the gossiper and her best friend Annabella, who happens to be one of the shyest people I know and barely utters a word," Ana blushed and looked down at her food. See what I mean about her being bashful? "And you also have a Goth." I ended my narration pointing at Greta whose black-painted lips turned up in a smirk. Are Goths supposed to smirk? "You are a very diverse crowd and that is pretty unique."

"We." Tara corrected. "You are a part of our group now, so it's "we are a very diverse crowd"."

"Yeah!" Joey agreed and I noticed a few people nodding. "We were lacking a delinquent chick in the group, so welcome to the posse!"

Looking around the table, I could see that everyone here shared that opinion. I smiled. So I got my own posse, huh? They were very different from the people I used to hang out with, but that was probably a good thing. I could get used to that; I could get used to being accepted by them. I just had to be careful not to scare them. And speaking of people I had to be careful around: I needed to find Tyson. I looked at the time on my phone; lunch would be over soon, but if I left now, than I could mosey along the school in hopes I'd bump into him.

"Guys, I heading out now. See you later!" To my surprise everyone responded with a friendly "bye" or a wave. As I was exiting the cafeteria all I could think about was: yep, I could get definitely get used to this!

*****

Tyson POV

I overslept and skipped the first few classes, coming to school at about lunch time. The hallways were pretty much empty as most people were in the cafeteria or eating outside in the courtyard. I was walking to my locker when it happened again.

"You are making a habit of running into me." I said to the little brunette who had just bumped into my chest. Looking her over, I noticed she was wearing all black again: black skinny jeans, black corset-like top, black leather jacket… I wondered if she had ever left the house without having something of that color on her.

"And you are making a habit of standing in my way." Alex wasted no time with her response, straightening her posture.

I kept on walking to my locker and she followed. What the heck did she want? I had no time to deal with her now. I had to get my things then drag my ass off to class, hoping I wouldn't get sent to the principle's office again for being absent so often. I was in no mood for the do-you-know-where-you-are-headed and the think-of-your-future speeches, I usually got while I was in there.

"How are you?" The girl asked.

I stopped to look at her puzzled by her question. Her face was completely blank except for some vague trace of indefinable emotion showing in her chocolate eyes.

"I'm fine." I answered cautiously, not sure where she was heading with her inquiries.

"When do you think we can have our fight?"

I smirked. So that's why the girl was asking. She seemed just as eager as me to bring it on. She was now done with hiding her feelings and was anxiously biting her lower lip whilst waiting for my reply.

"We can do it now if you want." I leaned on the nearby wall, ignoring the pain I still felt from my wounds and trying to look casual in hope she'll disregard her previous reserves. To my disappointment, Alex didn't.

"Not an option!" She stated unyieldingly.

"A few bruises won't make a difference; I'll still kick your ass," I protested, pushing myself off the wall a little too hastily, making some of my injuries ache.

"Maybe I should go to a doctor this time…" The thought passed through my mind, but I quickly dismissed it. I'd been through worse and survived without a specialist's help. I made sure not to display my pain and aimed my most daring, cocky smirk at the brunette.

"Ty, I told you: I'm not fighting you until you've healed."

I sighed heavily and started walking again. Stubborn little bitch. I could see how badly she wanted it. But I also saw she was determined not to row with me until I was better. It seemed she wouldn't take advantage of someone else's hardship and I guess I had to give the girl some credit for that. Where I came from, you'd rarely see such fair play. On the contrary, we were raised to use every weakness of our opponents for personal gain.

I stopped at my locker and I had to pound on it to get it open. The darn thing was always jammed.

"I can take a look at those by the way. I have some experience with wounds." The girl suggested and started fidgeting her silver locket. Was she nervous or something?

"I don't want your hands anywhere near me unless we're fighting." I cut her off bluntly. Didn't want her to think we could get chummy.

"Whatever!" Alex said with an eye-roll before leaving me on my own.

I took a notebook and a pen out of my locker and closed it. I didn't bother carrying textbooks with me. I rarely opened that stuff anyway. I headed for my next lesson – Biology. It was a pretty bearable class. The teacher, Mrs. Brown, was a decent woman and was quite patient with even the most difficult students. And by "the most difficult students" I meant mainly me.

I entered the room and saw there was only one more person there. She was sitting at the third desk in the middle row. I remembered I'd seen her at Alex's table at lunch yesterday. She was the one glaring at the short foreigner.

The moment the girl noticed me her expression changed from annoyance to one of temptation. Her green eyes lit up and she gave me a flirtatious smile while playing with a strand of her long black hair. I was used to such reactions by girls. They would sometimes shy away, blushing furiously or, if they were more confident, they would try to seduce me. But either way they would show some amount of romantic interest in me. Except for Alex of course. All she was interested in was fighting me. No romantic sentiments on her side. Why was that?

The black-haired girl's gaze followed me as I took a seat in the back next to the window. I tried to ignore her and looked outside. I had to admit: she was probably one of the most beautiful students here but I wasn't in a mood for flirts today. Actually, I rarely was. Although a lot of girls chased me around, very few had managed to catch my interest and excite me enough to make a move on them.

I heard the chatter of our classmates as they started filling the room. The teacher herself came in and our lesson began. Shortly after, there was a knock on the door. Alex entered and swiftly appraised Mrs Brown before giving the later a sheepish smile and saying politely:

"I'm sorry, Mrs Brown! I'm new and I kind of got lost."

It didn't escape my notice that the black-haired girl, who up till now was staring daggers at the short brunette, now rolled her eyes.

"She must really dislike Alex."

Not that I gave a damn about that.

"That's okay." The Mrs. Brown replied with an encouraging smile on her full lips. She looked beautiful when she did that. I know it was weird for me to say such a thing about someone much older than me (she was in her thirties or maybe even early forties), but it was true. I didn't have some high school crush on my teacher; I was simply pointing out a fact. "Please, take a seat!"

"Thank you!" Alex answered still genuinely smiling.

I raised my eyebrows. This was the first time I'd seen her being so civil to a teacher. I guess she must have really liked the woman.

Alex took a seat to my right again. I noticed she didn't put her headphones on. Instead, she concentrated on the lesson, taking down notes. After the class was over she even stayed behind to talk with Mrs Brown. I got so curious about her uncharacteristic behavior that I waited for the brunette outside of the classroom.

"Are you trying to ambush me?" Alex queried, closing the door on her way out.

Instead of answering her question, I asked one of my own:

"What was that about?"

"What do you mean?" She seemed confused.

"Your behavior. In the classroom."

"Oh, that!" She shrugged. "I liked the teacher. Plus it is a difficult subject for me and I have to keep my grades up for the scholarship."

"You get a scholarship?" I asked incredulous trough a bark of laughter. Her jaw clenched and her hands fisted. She appeared truly offended by my tone.

"Yes, I get a scholarship!" She snapped at me. "Believe it or not I do have a brain you know!"

And then she stalked away angrily.

*****

Gloriana POV

I came early to Biology. I was tired of listening to my "friends" praising that short bitch Allie. What was so special about her? The girl had no sense of fashion and her body wasn't even that good! She had small breasts. So why did boys even look at her? Guys like big boobs, just like mine. The way I dressed, my make-up and hairstyle - everything about me was carefully planned and carried out; I looked perfect! She barely wore any make-up, her hair looked terrible...

So why was it that Alexandra was getting all the attention the last two days? She was trying to steal my minions! Because that's what most of the people from my lunch group were – minions. They hung out with me because I was rich and beautiful and they liked the perks my popularity brought them. They were all so easy to manipulate! Except for that veracious girl Tara and her admirer Danny; those two were naïve, but smart. I wouldn't have them around but Tara's father and mine went to the same University and were business partners ever since they graduated. Dad always told me she was useful to keep an eye on. And where Tara went, Danny went. If that looser ever built up the courage to ask Tara out or vise versa, they'd form one of those disgustingly devoted couples that did everything together. Just the thought of their goofy, lovey-dovey grins made me sick to my stomach.

But Dan wasn't the only problem. Since Tara was nice to everyone, and I do mean everyone, all sorts of misfits grouped around her, including that total looser Anabella and that pain to my eyes Greta the Goth. What was the purpose of even talking to them? Of acknowledging their existence? I could understand keeping in touch with Isabella; she was so annoying that she gave me migraines, but she was a good source of information. Plus, I often used her to spread gossip for me. All I had to do was accidentally let slip some juicy tale of someone who had crossed me and she'd do my dirty work and spread the word around. The girl didn't even realize how often I made things up for the sole purpose of destroying someone's reputation. God, she was so easy to fool! Even more than the cheerleaders and they weren't known for their mental abilities. All they did was wave pompons around and drool over jocks like Mike Barbson and Joey, the latter being an annoyingly down to earth guy.

I sighed in irritation. God! The people one had to socialize with in order to keep their popularity! But being a cheerleader or a jock guaranteed you a place in the cool crowd, so I had to pretend I liked them.

"Well, at least the cheerleaders make good minions," I thought, examining my polished nails. I tilted my head up as I heard someone coming in the room.

It was Tyson Williams.

THE Tyson Williams! I've had my eyes on him for quite a while now but although he was one of the most popular (regardless of being notorious) guys at school, he wasn't a player. He didn't hook up at school, he rarely went to parties... Actually, did he even go to parties?

It was difficult for a girl to get him alone.

Difficult, but surely not impossible! And we were alone now...

I noticed Tyson looking at me and gave him my best flirtatious smile. I leaned forward and placed my breasts on the desk in order to give the boy a better view of what I had to offer. I swirled my hair around my finger. Yes, I knew all the tricks in the book and so much more. He headed in my direction and I could feel my excitement building. I smiled and bit my lower lip.

But he didn't stop. I scanned his body as he passed me by and took the opportunity to admire the nicely shaped ass this boy was the proud owner of. I thought that after he had given me a chance to appreciate both his front and back, he'd turn around and answer my unspoken flirt.

He did no such thing.

The boy kept on walking until he reached the back of the classroom, leaving me in an attempt to hide my irritation of being neglected. I wasn't used to such treatment! I wasn't used to be overlooked!

How dared he do that to me?

Now I wanted him even more.

He might be ignoring me at present, but he'll be mine soon!

CHAPTER FIVE - Future trouble

T yson POV

I was standing in front of a corner shop with seven guys, all of them at about my age. To someone passing us by, we would seem like a group of friends. But that person would be wrong.

These guys and I weren't really close because we all knew that with us it's every man for himself. I guess you could call us allies, forming a temporary fraction, until we move on to something better. I knew that none of them would hesitate to stab me in the back if they saw profit in that.

Yet those were the people I hung out with. You don't have much of a choice if you grow up where I did. Right now we were just chilling, smoking and drinking, and some of us chatting. I kept myself quiet as usual. I was leaning on the shop's wall and was just finishing my cig when I herd Bret wolf whistle.

"Well, well! Look what we have here, boys!" I heard him say. Bret fancied himself as a player, but he just seemed pathetic to me. His pick up lines were cheesy, his hair had so much gel on it that it looked like a petrol spill and he had the sleaziest smile I'd ever seen. His taste in women could be summed up as follows: not too ugly, not overweight and between the ages of fifteen and twenty-five; those were his only criteria and he sometimes ignored them, especially when he was drunk or high.

I didn't even turn to see who he was talking about this time.

"Aren't you a pretty little thing, girl!" This time it was Kent who spoke. Now this guy wasn't a waste of space, little slime ball like his subordinate Bret. Kent was street smart; he was more observing than the other boy, always cautious with his words and actions. His constant encounters with the law had thought him that much.

"Why don't you come here and have some fun with us?" He carried on speaking to whoever was the unlucky object of their interest.

"I seriously doubt you guys will be able to entertain me." I heard Alex's bored voice and my head snapped in her direction.

And there she was in all her five feet glory. Her hair was straightened and tied in a high ponytail. She wore no makeup except thick black eyeliner and maybe mascara. Alex was clad in a tight, strapless black top, short skirt that barely covered her ass and fishnets. With that and her two inch high, up-to-the-knee boots she pulled off the teenage hooker look like a pro.

What the hell was she thinking dressing up like that and coming to this neighborhood? Did she want to get raped?

Then again this was Alex; she probably thought she could just beat up anyone who tried to get their hands on her. And with her skills, she probably could.

The girl stood only about six feet away, but she hadn't noticed me yet as her eyes were trained on Bret and Kent. The look she gave them sent out the you-are-wasting-my-time-I-don't-want-anything-to-do-with-you message loud and clear and I was sure both boys got it.

But they decided to ignore it.

"Oh, I bet I can show you a good time!" Kent went on. "Here, why don't you have some of this?" He extended his hand with the unlit cigarette he had just rolled.

It was a joint.

"I don't think so," the girl replied, turning to the left and finally noticing me. "Yeah, sure! Why not run into you as well?" She rolled her eyes at me.

"I'm not exactly ecstatic to see you myself," I replied coolly.

"Tyson, you know the chick?" Bret asked me.

"We've met," Alex answered for me while looking straight into my eyes.

"I would stay away from this one, Bret. She's not worth the trouble." I glared at her.

"Did you just admit I'm too much for you to handle?" She smirked at me. I heard some of the boys snicker and Bret shouted "Burn!".

"No, I just said you're not worth wasting my time with you," I replied in irritation and lit another cigarette, feeling the sudden need to smoke again.

"Yeah, right!" She snorted, turning on her heel and walking into the store.

I took a long drag from my cig and exhaled slowly.

Why was it that this girl always managed to rub me up the wrong way? Her sole presence was enough to make me edgy.

"Hey, Tyson, who was that girl?" Kent queried with a calculating glint in his brown eyes.

It made me want to punch him. He had that look whenever he was plotting something and for some reason, I didn't like him aiming it at Alex.

"Just a bitch from my school," I answered vaguely, not wanting to tell him the little I knew about Alexandra.

He kept quiet for a while, with his eyes slightly narrowed. A few wrinkles formed on his forehead as the boy was obviously thinking something over.

What the hell was he scheming this time?

Even if Kent wanted to share his thoughts with me, he didn't get a chance to: just as he was about to speak again we saw a police car turn round the corner and stop not far away from us. The cops got out and headed for the store.

"Shit!" Kent cursed, quickly dumping the weed in an empty can behind him and leaning casually next to me. I tried to look relaxed as well and adopted a bored expression. Last thing I needed was to get arrested for possession; I didn't have that particular charge on my record and I planned on keeping it that way.

Bret on the other hand looked around trying to find a safe way to flee. He did not manage that, but he succeeded in gaining the officers' attention. They took us in and shook their heads disapprovingly.

"You boys stain' out of trouble?" The older one asked, his eyes darting between us before finally settling on Bret who (the idiot he was) glanced at Kent. The officer returned his gaze to the boy beside me, pretending he had only just noticed him. "Well, hello, Kent! You stayin' clean, boy?"

"Yes, sir!" Kent replied glaring in Bret's direction, annoyance clear in his gaze and voice. I swear, I sometimes though the only reason Kent put up with Bret's stupidity was because the later had on older brother who knew some very... useful people.

"Well, then you wouldn't mind me checking what you have in your pockets, would you, boy?" And with that the policeman approached us.

But before he could do anything, a piercing scream erupted from the store. Cursing, both cops ran inside with their guns pulled out. The guys and I stood there, staring at the door. Each of us was curious as to who produced that scream and why and finding that out was the only reason we didn't scatter when we had the chance.

A couple of minutes later the cops got out.

"A spider! A bloody spider!" The younger one was muttering "Can you believe this girl?"

"If I wasn't a cop, I'd shoot her myself," the older replied, getting in the car.

They drove away, apparently having forgotten all about us. Alex got out of the shop and watched them leave, a small self-satisfied grin gracing her lips. It didn't take a genius to figure out who had peeved the two officers.

"A spider?" I asked her while shaking my head.

"Hey, it got them of your back, didn't it?" She answered smugly. "You can get down on your knees and thank me any time you want!"

I was just about to tell her she could get on her knees and blow me, when Come Undone by My Darkest Days started playing and I reached for my phone at the same tine the brunette started rummaging through her black faux leather backpack. She took her mobile out and pressed the answering button.

"Yeah?" She replied with a bored voice. "Out." There was a short pause before she said: "Alone...ish," she added, glancing at us and scrunching her nose; apparently, the girl didn't like what she saw. She made a longer pause before going on:

"Why do you always…" She was starting to get irritated. She listened for a while before sighing heavily.

"I'm not lying…" She got interrupted again. "Fine, I lied! I am at the local whorehouse having an orgy with all the pimps and hookers!" She exclaimed angrily into the phone.

I heard some of my friends snicker to that while Bret's muttered "we can arrange the orgy" made me throw him a disgusted look. But although my companions enjoyed Alex's little outburst, the person on the other end of the line didn't seem to find it even a bit amusing and started shouting in her ear so loud, she had to hold the phone away from her. I could hear the words but they weren't in English so I couldn't understand what he was saying.

The girl started to absentmindedly play with a strand of her long hair, looking semi-bored and semi-vexed by the situation as if the whole thing had happened many times before. After a few minutes of shouting at her, the guy finally stopped, probably to take some air into his lungs.

"Relax, cousin! You know I was only joking. Would I really do that? Wait, don't answer that!" She waited while he said something else and sighed again. "Yeah, sure. I'll be there in forty or fifty minutes."

She ended the call and turned to us.

"Well, as fun as this little run into was," she started sarcastically, "I got places to be, people to meet… Bye!"

And with that she started to walk away while humming her ring tone. That reminded me it was also my ring tone.

"Why Come Undone?" I queried and saw her turning to face me.

"Why not?" She answered with a question of her own. "It's a good song. One of my favorites actually."

I snorted.

"Really? And here I thought Porn Star Dancing would be more your thing... Something you can relate to," I sneered.

"Perhaps." She admitted with a shrug of her shoulders and walked away.

I turned to the group of guys. All of them had their eyes on the departing girl's body, except for Kent. He was staring at me with that calculating glint in his eyes, the one that always meant trouble was coming, but before I could ask him what the fuck was his problem, we heard Alex singing.

Kelly won't kiss my friend, Cassandra

Jessica won't play ball

Mandy won't share her friend, Miranda

Doesn't anybody live at all?

I held back a smirk. The voice this girl used right now sounded pretty damn awesome: deep, sexy and raspy.

But I wasn't telling her that.

*****

A/N: I know the chapters so far were not very eventful and were mostly introductory, but from CHAPTER SIX onwards there will be more action and humor.

CHAPTER SIX - The babysitters

T yson POV

I walked into my best friend's house. I didn't bother to knock or ring the bell first. Angel and I have known each other for so long, I practically grew up here. His mom always welcomed me warmly to their home and made me feel like I was part of their family. I even had a key to their place.

"I'm so glad you came! Sorry for making you do this so often," he said from the kitchen. I followed his voice there and saw him rummaging through the fridge with his head hidden by the door.

"You know I don't mind." I really didn't. Growing up with Angel meant spending time with his little brother and two younger sisters. I didn't usually like children much but they were a pretty decent bunch. "You know I like your siblings."

"Yeah, about that... There has been a slight change of plan." That said, he poked his head from out of the fridge. "They are having a sleepover."

I froze at his words.

Oh, he better be joking!

"So, instead of one boy and two girls I'm babysitting...?"

"No boys; Jamie went over to his friend's house."

"And how many girls?" I was afraid of his answer.

"Six." He looked at me apologetically.

"What?! Angel, you want to leave me alone with six kids? With six girl kids?"

"I arranged for someone to come and help you out." He hurriedly tried to calm me down.

"Who? Don't tell me it's that chick two houses away. She always hits on me; it's pathetic!" He looked away nervously before hiding his head behind the fridge's door again. What was he doing there anyway? Digging for gold?

"Oh, it's a girl, but it's not her." He replied after a while.

"Really? Is she hot?" I asked on reflex. If I was to babysit six kids for him, the least my best friend could do was get me some eye candy.

"I believe I am if I can say so myself!" Alex's smug voice filled my ears.

"What the hell?" I snapped my head to the direction of the kitchen door. Short size, brown hair, a challenging look on her face... Yep, no mistake about it; it was her alright. "Angel, you've got to be fucking kidding me! You can't expect me to spend the whole night with her!"

"Can't spend the whole night with me, huh? What's the matter? Think you can't keep up, Williams?" She asked mockingly.

"Shut up, slut! Angel, you can't be serious!" I turned once again in my best friend's direction. I was practically whining by now.

"Sorry, but I am. You'll just have to make it work!"

If it was anyone else asking, I would've said "no". Hell, if it was anyone else asking, I wouldn't have come in the first place. But I knew how hard they had it being a family of four kids raised only by their mom: a woman who worked two jobs so she could take care of them. And me. Because no matter how short they were on money, she would always invite me to share their meal. Even when I got in trouble she didn't turn her back on me and gave Angel money to bail me out. I paid them back as soon as I could of course. I knew all that just as I knew Angel had to help out and go to work too.

Which is why I sometimes babysitted for him.

"Fine!" I growled. "But I can't guarantee we'll both be alive when you return."

"Same here." Alex's tone was much calmer than mine.

"Thanks, guys! You have no idea what this means to me." With those words he closed the fridge door (which I only now realized he had been using as an improvised wall of protection between him and I), took his jacket from one of the nearby chairs and left us.

"I can't believe he didn't warn us we will have to babysit together," I mumbled more to myself than to the nearby cocky brunette.

"Oh, he told me you'll be here." Her voice was surprisingly even.

"And you still agreed?" I asked incredulous. "Why?"

"Because I like him and I wanted to help him out. Simple as that."

A small, gentle smile appeared on her lips.

"So you're not getting anything out of it?"

"Nope." Her smile turned into a smirk. "Apart from pissing you off of course." And she exited the kitchen grinning like the Cheshire cat.

*****

All six of the girls were sitting on the floor (me being the only person on the couch) and they were watching some animated movie, called Tangled. Apparently they all liked it. Apparently so did Alex.

Yes, little miss I-kick-ass-so-stay-outta-my-way was a Disney fan. And just like those girls she had watched the movie before. And again just like those girls, she knew the songs and they were all singing and laughing and having the time of their life.

I myself was pondering which will be the quickest way to kill myself.

After what seemed like an eternity the movie finally ended and the credits rolled in.

"Just a few more minutes and this torture will be over!" I though and my lips formed into a relieved smile.

"She's the girl with the best intentions," the last song started.

"This is my favorite song from the movie!" Alex shouted, jumping excitedly from her seat on the floor.

"He's a man of his own invention," she sang along to the music.

"She looked out of window; he walked out the door," Alex did a little swirl here. "But she followed him and he said "Whatcha you looking for"?"

Now she started jumping and swirling around haphazardly with a huge grin on her face while singing:

"And she said "I want something that I want. Something that I tell myself I need Something that I want...""

The six little girls joined her "dance" with unadulterated enthusiasm. God, their singing would be the death of me! It wasn't even singing; it was more like squealing. Even Alex was just shouting the lines, not bothered whether she sounded good or not.

"...Right when you think, you know what to say,someone comes along and shows you a brand new way." At that part our eyes connected and I saw her smile at me before quickly averting her eyes. A real smile, not a sarcastic grin or a smug smirk, but a genuine smile that caught me completely off guard.

"... it's so easy to make believe," here her voice became more gentle and actually sounded pretty good. "Seems you're living in a dream," she continued with her eyes closed.

"Don't you see that what you need

is standing in front of you"

She had a serene, dreamy expression on her face and I just couldn't look away from her.

"I want something that I want..."

The song went on and the brunette opened her eyes but there was still a faraway look in them that made her look just so... gentle.

Somehow the song didn't seem to be bothering me any more.

*****

"One more time! One more time!" Jinny, Angel's youngest sibling squealed excitedly. I groaned.

She wanted to listen to the final song again? It was on repeat for the last fifteen fucking minutes!

"Alex, please let's listen to it again!" Tina, who was second eldest after Angel and in her early teens, pleaded.

"Okay!" Alex agreed and I was just about to protest when she went on: "But this is the last time and then you're going to sleep." The girls seemed like they wanted to protest so she quickly added with a stern tone: "Not negotiable! It's already past your bedtime anyway." And with that she turned the damn song on again.

The moment it begun all the girls started dancing. Tina, Jinny and one other girl, whose name I didn't remember, were holding hands while jumping around. Suddenly, the girls lost their balance and all three of them fell, pushing the table and spilling the drinks and what was left of the popcorn on the floor, on the couch and (since I was still sitting there) by association on me.

"Oh, fuck!" I screamed, abruptly jumping up.

All of the girls gasped while Alex gave me a criticizing look.

"Are you guys okay?" She questioned the three girls that had fallen. They all nodded.

"Sorry about the mess!" Tina said apologetically.

"We'll help you clean up," Jinny added.

"Don't worry about it!" Alex smiled reassuringly. "But since the couch is now wet we'll have to alter the sleeping arrangements." She went on thoughtfully. A small crease formed on her forehead and she pouted slightly. It looked kind of adorable on her.

Adorable? Seriously? What was wrong with me tonight?

She was right about having to change our plans though. Angel's house had four single beds for the kids and one double for their mom. The plan was for three of the girls to sleep on the double, Alex and the other three girls on the singles and I on the couch.

Well, that was obviously out now.

"I'll think of something," the brunette muttered and then turned to me. "Why don't you go clean yourself up? I'll take care of things here."

I nodded and went to one of the bathrooms. I took my singlet off; it was completely drenched. I washed the soda and draped the clothing to dry on a rope they had hung in the bathroom. By the time I got out the girls were gone and Alex was just finishing cleaning up the mess they've made.

"So what's the plan?" I queried.

"We connected the two singles in the girls' room so they would fit in Jinny, Tina and one more girl and we did the same to the beds in the boys' room for the rest of the girls." She briefly explained to me.

"And where are we sleeping?"

"On the double."

"What?" I croaked. "Both of us?"

"Unless you want to sleep on the floor." She answered, her tone even.

I just stood there, staring at her, searching for a sign to tell me she was joking. There was none. She stared back with her face completely drained out of any emotion. After a few minutes of silence she sighed tiredly and asked:

"So what did you decide? Are you sleeping with me or not?"

"Am... I... Wh-what?" I stuttered.

"What's the matter? Never slept with a girl before?" She questioned confused, a small crease forming on her forehead. When I didn't answer her teasing grin appeared. "Oh, my, oh, my! Do my ears deceive me? Have the oh-so-sexy highly-wanted Tyson Williams never slept with a girl before?"

"I've had sex with girls," I growled in her direction. For some reason I didn't want her to think I was completely inexperienced.

"That's not what I asked, is it?" She was grinning like the Cheshire cat again. "You don't have to fuck a girl to sleep in the same bed with her. Or is it just me that makes you uneasy?"

"Don't flatter yourself, slut!"

"Hey, you're the one who started stammering the moment I mentioned us sleeping together. I don't have problem sharing a bed."

"Oh, I bet you don't. I bet you are quite used to sharing your bed with other people."

"And what will be so wrong with that?" She asked huskily, taking a few steps towards me. "What will be wrong with having a little fun with a boy... or a girl... or both? I mean, why choose when you can have both, right?"

She took a few more steps towards me and I moved back until I felt the wall hitting my back. Alex didn't stop moving until she was standing directly in front of me. She gently put her hands on my naked chest and stared straight into my eyes. I gulped. She smiled and leaned forward, standing on her tiptoes.

"Tyson..." She breathed seductively into my ear. "Do you want to fuck me, Tyson?" She pulled back slightly to look at my face. I stared at her eyes. There was a playful glint to them. My eyes fell to her lips; always slightly open and so terribly inviting. She bit her lower lip and I licked mine. The little smirk she had on grew wider at my gesture.

"You do want me, don't you, Tyson?" Her husky voice reached my ears.

Tyson.

She rarely called me by my name and now she was repeating it over and over again. I liked that. I liked the way she pronounced my name. And the look in her eyes right now? Well, it definitely had an effect on a certain part of me. I was breathing irregularly and felt slightly light-headed.

"Alex..." I whispered and was surprised by how raspy my voice sounded. I tried to steady it before I continued. "Get the fuck away from me, bitch!" I commanded quietly.

She burst out laughing.

"Damn! For a moment there I thought I had you." She said when she finally calmed down.

"Did you really think such cheap tricks on your part will have any effect on me?" I attempted to keep my voice even and tried to sustain eye contact; if the girl looked bellow my waist now, she'd realize her tactics definitely had the effect she had been after.

"They might be cheap tricks but I'm good at them." She sounded slightly offended. "So... what did you decide? Am I spreading myself on the whole bed or are we cuddling?"

"Neither. I'm sharing the bed, but if you touch me..."

"Don't worry about it," she cut me off. "I was just messing with you. Although I might be tempted to smother you with your pillow." She said, heading upstairs.

"If I don't get you first." I muttered, following suit.

CHAPTER SEVEN - Put some pants on

T yson POV

Alex was changing in the bathroom, leaving me to stand alone and ponder whether I should sleep only in my boxers like I usually did or keep my jeans on. Thinking that I'm not going to be comfortable in jeans (and more important: that Alex will mock me if I keep them on), I decided to go for the former. Unbuttoning them, I quickly slipped the dark blue fabric off and jumped into the bed, covering myself with the light comforter. A moment later Alex came in wearing a Guns N Roses t-shirt that was several sizes too big for her small frame. It reached mid thigh and the collar was so wide that it slid slightly over her left shoulder. From what I could tell she wasn't wearing any pants. Not even shorts.

"You seem to have forgotten part of your clothing," I stated coolly.

"Ha, ha!" Was her sarcastic reply.

"Are you going to sleep in only that?" I persisted. It would be really distracting having her pants-less in the same bed. Hell, that would be distracting even if she had a whole bunch of clothes on her!

"That is what I usually sleep in." She grinned wickedly at me. "Does it bother you?"

"Don't care."

"Mhmm." She didn't look convinced by my statement as she climbed into bed and snuggled under the comforter.

My comforter.

I froze.

"What are you doing?" I shot out a bit too quickly.

"What does it looks like I'm doing?" She asked irritated. "I'm tucking myself in."

"Why with my comforter?"

"Because it's the only one in the room," she stated with a duh voice.

I lifted my head up and scanned the bedroom. Nope, no other comforter in sight!

"Why didn't you get another one?" I queried.

"Because I completely forgot about you when I was taking it from Angel's room."

"Idiot," I muttered.

"Hey, I'm letting you share the comforter I got for myself; show some appreciation!"

"Appreciation? Here, take it all! I don't need it!" I stated, tucking myself out of the covers and pushing them towards her.

"Well, the view definitely improved," she purred.

I looked at Alex in confusion. Then I saw the way she was watching me. Or to be more specific, the area including my abs. I remembered I was lying in the bed next to her in only my boxers. Suddenly I felt self-conscious and heat flooded my cheeks. I wasn't one to blush, but for some reason the way this girl was taking my body in made me glad that she had turned off the lights when she came in the room. The light from outside was enough for her to still see me, but not to register the fact that my face was getting redder by the minute. That was if she ever bothered looking away from my body and at my face instead.

"How long do you plan on staring?" I croaked out.

"How long do you plan on standing only in your boxers?" She teased.

"You're a slut, Alex," I stated, covering myself with the comforter once again and turning my back to her. I heard her chuckle quietly before she said:

"Sweet dreams, Tyson!"

There was softness in her voice and I could not figure out why her mood had altered so quickly. It was a pleasant change though.

"Sweet dreams!" I whispered back, half-hoping she wouldn't hear me. Hearing her chuckle again, I knew that she had.

*****

I was lying on my side and something was wrapped around the upper part of my thigh. Too lazy to open my eyes yet, I ran my hand over it, enjoying the soft and smooth texture. I was still sleepy and it took me a while to figure out that it was a leg. It felt good having it wrapped around my body. My hand stopped mid-stroke and my whole body tensed when I remembered where I was and whose was the leg that I was patting. I hesitantly opened my eyes, preparing myself to see the teasing smirk she no doubt had for me.

But it wasn't there.

During the night I must have turned in the bed because instead of being greeted by the wall, I was staring straight into Alex's blissfully asleep form. I took in the view before me.

Her hair was messy and part of it fell in her face. The natural reddish highlights were showing again because of the sunlight falling over her head. Her body was curled up close to mine with her right leg wrapped loosely around me. The shirt she slept in had gone up revealing the bottom of her flat stomach and a pair of silky black panties with red lace at the edges. I gulped and licked my lips at the sight of them. Memories of the evening before when this girl was mock seducing me flooded my mind.

I remembered the touch of her hands on my bare chest: it was so light that it was only teasing; I remembered the sweet seductive voice and the playful glint in her eyes; I remembered the way she purred my name... Tyson. God, the effect her voice had on me! I didn't want to admit it but it was such a turn on! Even now when I was just recollecting the scene I could feel a certain part of me below the waist perk up. I closed my eyes and groaned quietly.

"Great! Just what you needed!" A little voice inside my head reprimanded. "You can't lust after her; you hate this little bitch! She's caused you nothing but trouble. You know she's only doing this to confuse you. You can't let her get under your skin!"

"And I won't!" I promised myself.

I heard her moan sleepily and felt her shuffle in the bed. My eyes snapped open when she placed her head and one of her hands on my chest.

Was this just another joke of hers? Was she doing it on purpose?

I looked closely at the girl; she appeared to still be asleep. I couldn't be sure though - Alex was tricky.

"Alex?" I called her name quietly. No answer.

"Alex!" I repeated louder this time. She furrowed her eyebrows and groaned slightly, but still didn't open her eyes.

"Alex!" I all but shouted now.

She slowly opened her eyes, trying to focus.

"You are not my pillow," the brunette accused.

"Thanks for letting me know!" I retorted sardonically. "I was getting confused."

"You're welcome!" And with that she closed her eyes again without moving away from me.

"Why the fuck are you lying on me?"

"For somebody with so little fat to their body, you're actually really comfy, you know that?" I had a feeling she was trying to hold back a smirk. "Besides, Ty, from what I can very clearly feel you seem to be enjoying it," she stated, slightly thrusting her hips and brushing against my privates.

I pushed myself away from her so fast that I rolled off the bed and fell to the floor with a loud cuss. I heard her bark a laugh.

"That's a guys' thing that happens in the morning. It doesn't have anything to do with you!" I shouted at her. Technically it wasn't a lie although her presence didn't help the matter.

"I know, I know, I was just messing with you again." She said, prying her head from the bed's end and looking down at me still lying on the floor. Her gaze trailed from my face down to the area below my waist. "Although it would've been flattering if that was for me." She gave me a wink and got up. "Now put some pants on; there are little kids in the house!"

"Same goes to you." I remarked, getting up.

"It's okay; they are all girls and so am I."

Nonetheless, she put on her jeans, keeping the over-sized t-shirt on.

"Aren't you going to put on a bra?" I asked dryly while getting dressed as well.

"Nope. I like to keep the peaches free." She glanced down at her "peaches". "Plus, they are small so they don't provide much of a distraction, right?" She added in a mockingly innocent tone.

Small but perky it would seem.

But I kept that comment to myself.

*****

Alex was making pancakes for breakfast. She was actually pretty good at it. She was making them "the Bulgarian way" as she put it: really thin, almost see-through, but didn't let a single one burn because she was constantly flipping them over by throwing them in the air. By the time she was done, Angel was already back from his night shift so the three of us and the six little girls were currently seated in the kitchen, munching on the food.

"Thanks again for babysitting, guys!" Angel said, getting up to clean the dishes once we were done eating. "And for making breakfast," he added, leaning down and pecking Alex on the cheek. She smiled up at him and at the same time a sharp brief pang ran through me.

Must be from the pancakes!

The doorbell rang and shortly after one of the girls was called. Her parents had come to take her home. In less than half an hour all four of them were picked up. Tina and Jinny went upstairs to play, leaving Alex, Angel and I alone on the first floor.

"So how was babysitting?" Angel asked, sitting on the couch. Alex sat beside him and placed her legs in his lap.

Slut!

I glared at them from one of the sofas.

"Much better than I had expected!" Alex admitted.

"Speak for yourself! Angel, they made me watch Tangled!" I whined.

"You actually succeeded in making Tyson Williams watch Tangled?" Angel asked Alex, amazed by her achievement.

"No, I succeeded in making him stay in the room when we watched it while he probably contemplated suicide," she stated proudly.

"Damn movie!" I muttered.

"It's not that bad!" My friend stated. He had probably watched it with his siblings before. "The part with the thugs was pretty fun."

"Yeah!" Alex agreed "And then there's Pascal... Oh, and Max!"

"Oh, that horse was sick..."

They kept on talking about the characters and laughing at their favorite lines until I couldn't take it anymore and cleared my throat meaningfully.

"So what else happened while I was working?" Angel queried, attempting to change the topic.

"Nothing much," Alex replied. "Oh, the girls spilled some soda on the couch, but I cleaned it up."

"Then where did you sleep?" He questioned, turning to me.

Once again the girl cut me off and answered for me, explaining how we changed the sleeping arrangements.

"You guys slept together?" My best friend asked incredulous.

"Not together, just in the same bed," I responded somewhat defensively.

"Apparently he finds the idea of having sex with me completely repulsive," Alex remarked sourly.

"I don't know what I might catch from you," I shot back.

"What's that suppose to mean?"

"Only that you'd fuck anything human!"

"Um, guys..." Angel tried to interrupt our bickering.

"Hey, I have standards!" She protested, getting her legs off of Angel's lap and twisting her body so she could angle herself to look at me better.

"Guys..." I could barely hear Angel's cautious tone.

"What standards?" I asked sardonically. "Breathing?"

"I'm just gonna leave you alone to deal with it," my best friend said, getting up and heading to his room upstairs.

"Ha-ha! Very funny, Tyson! You're such a comedian... NOT! And how the fuck would you know how many people I've screwed?" Alex glared furiously at me.

"I know your type!"

"Oh, really? And what is my type?"

I got up and stood in front of her. I placed my hands on either side of her on the couch and leaned my face down so that our eyes were on the same level. I locked my gaze with hers before answering as calmly as I could.

"You like to toy with people's minds. You do that by using their lust against them. You flirt around and if that isn't enough to get what you want from them, you fuck around. You're nothing but a pretentious selfish little slut, who thinks she could have people eat from the palm of her hand only because she has a pretty face and a hot body."

"Wow!" She exclaimed quietly. "You make me sound like the Devil himself."

"No, just his daughter."

"That's kind of flattering," the girl smirked. "Having superhuman power, I mean."

"It wasn't a compliment," I growled at her.

"Too late; I already decided to take it as one."

We stayed in silence for a while just staring at each other.

"Do I have that effect on you as well?" She asked me.

"Hmm?"

"Do I have such power over you as to make you eat out of the palm of my hand?" She questioned, a playful inflection to her voice.

"Don't be absurd!"

"Am I being absurd, Tyson?" She literally purred my name, just like the night before, and placed her hands on top of my palms.

The girl moved her arms slowly up, brushing them against mine, until finally she hooked them behind my neck. Her eyes closed slightly, giving her a seductive look as she gazed up at me through her thick eyelashes. I felt my breathing pick up speed.

What the hell?

It was this very morning that I had promised myself not to let Alex get under my skin. And yet here I was, breaking that promise. She was barely touching me but it was enough to turn me on. But I guess it wasn't just her touch; she was taunting me with her voice and captivating me with her eyes. My gaze fell on her lips.

What would they taste like? Would they be as soft as they looked?

There was one way to find out. I felt myself leaning forward slightly but I sobered up before I completely closed the distance between our lips.

That would've been a mistake.

"You'll never have me eating out of the palm of your hand!" I spat out.

"Never say never!" She grinned, cocking one eyebrow up before unhooking her hands and exiting the room, leaving me alone with my thoughts.

That was close! That was too close! What was wrong with me? I had more self-control around girls. Then again I haven't gotten laid in a while. Yeah! That must be it! That must be the reason!

I needed to get laid!

CHAPTER EIGHT - First Restricted Chapter

This chapter is actually an excerpt of the previous one, but due to mature content, I'll post it as a separate story, under the title "Here We Go Again - Restricted".

For those of you who don't like or consider themselves too young for R-rated stories - don't worry, you can skip chapter 8 WITHOUT missing out on the plot; it's just a one page description of one of the main characters having a good time.

In "Here We Go Again - Restricted" I'll be putting all parts of "Here We Go Again" that are for a mature audience and yes, I'll give an announcement like this one each time I do this.

Click on the External Link and you'll be directed to Here We Go Again - Restricted or type 20661720 in the discover bar and click Enter.

CHAPTER NINE - Nice Alex and Mean Alex

A /N: "Da" means "yes".

*****

Alex POV

I was in the bad part of the town again. I knew I shouldn't be here, but I couldn't help myself. I missed the excitement in my life. Ever since I moved here I've stayed out of trouble. Well, apart from my fight with Tyson.

Tyson Williams.

One of the stars at the Ring. The boy was so good I'd heard of him all the way back home. Then again I used to roll with people connected to the Ring there.

The Ring was something like a... hmm... let's just say it gave opportunities to make money. How you might ask? By providing a cop-free space for people to beat the crap out of each other under the ravenous applause of the crowd. Yes, the Ring was all about illegal fighting and the gambling that went along with it.

It was sort of an international chain with its own set of rules. No weapons or metal objects were allowed. The idea was to make a show, but whoever ran it didn't want to leave corpses behind. From what I'd heard, they had quite a few cops in their pockets, but leaving a bloody trail was still not the smartest thing to do.

Of course there were the occasional slip-ups. And if things got too intense with the coppers, the Ring would simply disappear from that town.

I wondered for how long had Tyson worked there.

Speak of the devil! I just keep on running into that boy, don't I?

*****

Tyson POV

The small figure was far, but I knew without a doubt it was Alex. So she came back here? Was she looking for me? Did she come to fight me? I hadn't told her I lived around. But she could've heard that from someone at school. She could've heard that from Angel.

"One way to find out I guess!" I thought, approaching her. She had also noticed me and was coming my way.

"What the fuck are you doing here?" I less-than-politely greeted.

"Decided to take a walk." She shrugged.

"In this neighborhood?"

"What's the matter? Worried about me?" She teased with a playful glint in her chocolate eyes.

"As if." I snorted. "I'm just sick of seeing you everywhere I go."

"Then stop looking!" She threw her hands in the air exasperated, all signs of her previous blithe behavior gone.

"Don't tell me what to do!"

"I will, if I want to!" She replied taking a step towards me.

"No, you won't!" I moved forward as well.

"Yes, I will!" She got even closer and flashed me one of her signature challenging glares.

I was sure we sounded like two little kids bickering right now. Regardless of that, I wasn't backing down. No way was I going to let this girl win anything against me, even a dumb, childish quarrel.

"No, you won't!" I snarled again.

"Yes, I will!" Alex hissed back.

We stared at each other and excitement ran through me as I knew the moment had come. At last! We were going to finish what we started weeks ago. And then we heard them again.

Those darn sirens!

I started running in the direction of my house. I was furious. I couldn't believe we got interrupted again. And once more by those fucking sirens. It wasn't so unusual in this neighborhood but still!

Arriving at my destination, I finally slowed down.

The porch boards creaked as I walked on them and reached with my right hand for my keys. Only my hand was already holding something... another hand. A small, pale, feminine hand with darkly polished fingernails. I looked at its owner's face.

"What the fuck are you doing here?" I asked her for a second time tonight.

Alex burst out laughing. She had an obnoxiously loud laugh for a girl!

*****

Alex POV

"You mean to tell me you really didn't realize you were dragging me with you?" I questioned with humor in my voice. He probably didn't want to admit it because all he said was:

"Go. Away!" I didn't move. "Didn't you hear me?"

"Oh, I heard you," I answered amused. "But you're still holding my hand captive."

His face turned red from embarrassment. He looked kind of ... cute like that.

"Oh, you're blushing!" I teased him. "How... adorable!"

His face turned even redder.

"Don't ever..." Tyson hissed, leaning slightly to my face in a threatening manner "... EVER call me adorable!"

He spat out the last word. Well, at least he didn't deny the blushing.

"Now get lost!" He snarled at me, letting go of my limb.

"What? Aren't you going to invite me in?" I asked innocently. "And I really, really wanted to see your bedroom." I stated through a sigh, shaking my head in fake disappointment. Or maybe not that fake: I was curious as to how this boy's room would look.

"Beat it!" He seemed angrier than before.

"Well, I guess I'm not getting a field trip into Ty's world tonight," I thought and turned on my heals, but managed to take only one step before the boy grabbed me again.

"Shit!" He cussed. I looked back and saw him staring at a car that had just turned round the corner and was coming our way. I couldn't make out the exact model from this far, but I noticed it was an old, beat-up vehicle.

"I guess you'll get your wish after all," Tyson stated bitterly, before pushing me rather violently into his house.

*****

Tyson POV

"Beat it!" I was getting angrier by the minute.

Alex actually turned to leave. Yes! Miracles do happen! I looked up and saw the all too familiar car approaching. Before the girl could move away I clutched her arm again.

"Shit!" I muttered. She looked at me with confusion and I tried to make my face unreadable.

"I guess you'll get your wish after all." I said before pushing her into the house and rushing her upstairs.

I wasn't sure why I'd done that. I guess I just didn't want her to be seen by the driver of that car - my father. My "sperm donor" was closer to the truth because he was never a real dad to me.

Why did he have to come back tonight? I hadn't seen him in weeks and I was hoping to turn that into months.

I pushed open the door to my room and made a gesture with my hand for Alex to go in first. Surprisingly, she obeyed and I followed her, closing the door behind us. I waited for her to query as to why I was doing this: that seemed like a natural thing, given the circumstances. But the girl appeared to be waiting for me to bring it up as she kept silent.

"I'm not telling you why I did this." I finally spoke firmly. "But I have my reasons. Trust me: you better sleep here tonight than go downstairs."

I knew he was already in the house; I could hear him moving around on the first floor. He wasn't even trying to keep quiet as he was bumping into furniture, too drunk to keep his balance. With each collision, he'd let out a cuss.

"So let me get a few things straight," Alex started, looking at me dead in the eye and studiedly ignoring the sounds from downstairs. "Number one: you can't stand me. Number two: you don't want to see me. Number three: regardless of numbers one and two, you want me to sleep in your room. And number four: you won't even explain why. Am I getting this right?"

"Pretty much." I muttered, realizing how idiotic that sounded.

"Oh!" She kept quiet for a while and gazed around the room. "Since I'm a guest I get the bed, right?"

"What?"

"Apparently I'm sleeping here tonight and since you're the host and there is only one single bed, I'm using it, right?"

I stared at her. She agreed? She actually agreed? I thought she was going to protest and start a fight; something I didn't want for once. But no; all she said was "Oh".

"Are you out of your mind?" I couldn't help but asking. "How can you agree to this so easily after you have so many reasons not to?"

"Did you want me to disagree with you?"

"No. But I expected you to!"

"And I usually would've but you seem to have your reasons. Besides, we've already slept in the same room when we were babysitting. So the way I see it, it's pretty simple: I'm staying here."

"Just like that?"

"Da. Just like that."

*****

Alex POV

I was listening to the verbal battle between the voices in my head.

It started with me feeling guilty about letting Tyson sleep on the hard floor while I was tucked in his bed. It wasn't the best of beds, but it was still better than where he was currently lying. I was just about to offer him to join me when one of the voices said:

"Let the boy suffer! He practically kidnapped you!" Mean Alex ordered.

"Or maybe he saved you from whoever is downstairs." Nice Alex contradicted.

I thought about that. I had a suspicion that whoever was driving that car was the same person currently resigning on the first floor. A parent perhaps?

Mean Alex: "Does it really matter? Even if he is trying to protect you, he is still the same self-centered asshole!"

Nice Alex: "How can he be a self-centered asshole if he is both protecting her and offering her his bed?"

Nice Alex had a point. It was not fair for him to sleep there after being nice to me. Well, as nice as Tyson Williams can be.

Mean Alex: "I can't believe you're still even considering that!"

Nice Alex: "She is considering it because unlike you she actually has a conscience. Just like me."

Mean Alex: "Listen here, bitch! I got our girl out of trouble plenty of times without you and your overrated conscience!"

Nice Alex: "Oh, yeah? Thanks to me she made friends – real friends, ones she can depend on!"

"Girls, we're getting off topic here!" I scolded.

I heard Tyson groan and shift on the floor. Nice Alex seemed to have won: I was going to offer him to join me.

Mean Alex: "If he's joining you then at least fuck him; the boy's hotter than Hell!"

Mean Alex, you're a slut!

"Hey, Ty?" I called out quietly. "Why don't you join me in bed?"

CHAPTER TEN - I want some waffles

T yson POV

"Hey, Ty?" Alex's quiet voice reached my ears. "Why don't you join me?"

I opened my eyes and saw her hesitantly peaking from the edge of my bed. It reminded me of the time when we were at Angel's house; she was on the bed looking down at me lying on the floor. I remembered how I got there. And more specifically – why I got there. I recollected how she ground against me just once and how my body responded to that. What if she tried something similar now?

"I'm fine," I responded in a low voice.

"I promise I won't come onto you tonight."

"I said I'm fine!" I snapped at her, getting peeved that she figured out why I wanted to stay away from her.

"Fine! Have it your way then!"

Alex got up from the bed, taking the pillow and covers with her. I watched her in confusion as she placed one sheet on the floor next to me and lied down covering herself with the other.

"What are you doing?" I asked the girl.

"If you're not sleeping on the bed, then neither am I!"

"Why not?"

"Chyvstvam se vinovna," she muttered.

"What?"

"I said... Never mind! Go to sleep!"

"Alex?" She didn't respond and just closed her eyes. "Alex!" She fake-snored. "Alex, I know you're awake!" She snored again, only louder this time. "Damn it, Alexandra! Stop getting on my fucking nerves and answered my darn question!"

"I said I was feeling guilty... You know, for occupying your bed while you are on the floor," she responded, not opening her eyes. She seemed almost shy to admit it.

So this girl actually had a conscience, huh?

I thought about the whole situation. There was no point in both of us sleeping down here and leaving the bed empty. True, it was a single bed, but with Alex being so small, she wouldn't take up much space. And she did promise to leave me alone.

I sighed.

"Okay! We're both using the bed." I finally agreed, getting off the floor.

*****

The first thing I saw when I woke up the next morning was the still asleep and snoring (this time for real) Alex. I tried to contain my laughter when I saw her.

Her hair was a mess. Her head was tilted to the side and her mouth was gapping wide. She had twisted her body in the most unbelievable and probably spine-breaking position with her right hand covering her head and her left leg dangling off the bed. She was lying on her stomach and the pillow had somehow managed to get under it. The bed covers were now lying in a ball on the floor.

It's got to be one of the most comical sights I've ever seen!

"Alex," I called her softly. I frowned, noticing the tone of my voice.

Why was I so nice today?

"Alex!" I said less tenderly and shook her.

She groaned.

"I can't go to school today, Kevin; I'm sick!" She let out an unconvincing cough.

Who's Kevin?

"I'm not making you go to school. It's Saturday."

"Oh! I'm fine then," she replied sleepily. "I'm still not getting up though." Her forehead wrinkled as if she was trying to comprehend something. "Wait... Tyson?" Her eyes opened slowly and gazed into mine. "Why the fuck did you wake me up?"

"I was going to ask you if you wanted me to make you breakfast."

"Breakfast?!" Alex exclaimed excitedly, opening her eyes wider. "Why are you still here? Go make me a sandwich!" She ordered.

"You better be kidding!" I growled at her tone. I knew I shouldn't have been nice!

"Of course I'm kidding. I'm not in a mood for having sandwiches for breakfast today. Now go make me a waffle on the waffleler!"

"On the WHAT?"

"Waffleler? Wafflemaker? Whatever that thing that makes waffles is called. Angel told me you have one."

I looked at her amused.

"Say "waffleler" again!" I demanded.

"Why?" She asked with suspicion clear in her voice.

"You sound really..." cute (was what I thought), "... funny" (was what I voiced instead).

"No, I don't!" She pouted.

"Yes, you do. You can't pronounce "r" correctly so it sounds like "waf-flelew"."

"Whatever, I'm not saying it!"

"Say it or I won't make you waffles!"

She glared at me, but I noticed a hint of amusement in her eyes.

"Do you blackmail all of your guests or should I feel special?" She tried to look peeved, but I could see the edges of her mouth lifting slightly to form a smile.

"I try that with everybody but it only works on the hungry ones." I winked at her.

Next thing I know, Alex burst out laughing, falling off the edge of the bed.

*****

The uncharacteristically good mood I woke up in left me the moment I went downstairs. I searched for signs of my father but couldn't find any. He wasn't in his usual place: passed out drunk on the couch in front of the TV. I gazed through the window; his car was gone.

Probably went to buy more booze.

How he managed to drive was beyond my understanding. He was never sober, he just had different levels of being drunk. There was sober-ish (when he only had a few beers), slightly drunk (add a few more), drunk, very drunk, not-being-able-to-move-but-still-relatively-awake drunk and (my favorite) passed-out-cold drunk. I rarely saw him at level one or two. Then again I did my best to avoid him whenever it was possible.

I heard a noise and saw Alex coming down the stairs. She hadn't change back into her clothes and was only dressed in an old black button up shirt of mine that I gave her to sleep in. She looked good wearing my clothes.

Whoa, Tyson, keep those thoughts out of your head!

"You're taking too long with breakfast," she complained, looking at my face before turning away to survey my house.

Suddenly, I felt edgy. This place was a shit hole. Everything was old, cheap and dirty. It had old, mostly broken, cheap furniture and old cheap torn wallpapers that had lost their colors years ago. To top it all up, it smelled of cheap alcohol and cheap cigarettes. It usually didn't bother me; I grew up here, I was used to it. But right now I was anxious to see Alex's reaction. Her face was blank.

"Well?" I questioned bitterly. "How do you like my five star residence?" I swung my hands as if I was showing the place off.

"It's a house." Alex said evenly.

"I know it's a house. But don't you think it's a beautiful one?" I asked sarcastically.

"Tyson, we both know this place sucks."

"Don't know what you're talking about; I personally find it's very charming and cozy!" I kicked one of the empty beer cans that were scattered around the floor. "Just look at all the lovely furniture!" I added sardonically, pointing at the old, stained couch and sofas and the rickety table, tilted to its side due to the lack of two of its legs.

Alex took a deep breath and released it slowly.

"What do you want me to say, Ty? Obviously you didn't like me not saying anything. Obviously you wouldn't like it if I gave some compliment without meaning it. And now you are sulking because I told the truth and didn't sugarcoat it for you?"

"What can I say; I'm a hard to please boy," I replied tartly.

"What a coincidence! I'm a hard to please girl," she used the same sharp tone of voice as me and then sighed again. "So does the waffle offer still stand?"

I stared at her in disbelief. We were quarreling a moment ago and now she was asking for breakfast? What the hell?! I was just about to tell her to go fuck herself when I took in her demeanor. That look on Alex's face... did she change the topic to try to calm me down?

"Are you trying to distract me?" I queried coolly.

"Not working, huh?" She gave me a sheepish smile. "Look, Ty... I don't want you to be upset because then you'll just chase me away. And believe it or not I... Well, as irritating as you can be... And trust me: you are really, really irritating sometimes... But regardless, I... That is you..."

"Alex, you're babbling," I noted evenly.

She took another deep breath.

"Mamka my!"

I wasn't sure what that meant, but I suspected it was a cuss.

"I don't know..." Alex went on. "I guess I just... I guess I like having around somebody on my level to fight with. To bring some excitement as oppose to knowing for sure that I'm going to win. Yeah, I guess that's what I meant..."

Seeing Alex's cheeks redden as she spoke I couldn't help but let out a chuckle. She was just so cute!

"So how many waffles do you want?" I asked, turning my back to her and walking towards the kitchen.

"Depends on how big your waff..." She caught herself before she could let it slip, "... waffle-maker is."

"Come and see for yourself!" I gestured for her to follow me. "Oh! And, Alex?"

"Mhmm?"

"It's nice to have you around to fight with too!"

My good mood was back.

*****

Alex POV

I was sitting on Tyson's kitchen counter. I didn't trust the chairs; they looked like they would brake any moment now. Tyson himself was washing the dishes we used during breakfast. I offered to help him clean up but to my immense relief, he declined. Washing dishes had always been my most hateful chore.

As he put the last dish on the dryer, the boy leaned on the counter next to me, angling his body so he could face me.

We'd had quite a peaceful breakfast. We hadn't argued a single time and just joked around. I didn't even know the boy had a sense of humor and it was a pleasant discovery.

I smirked at the thought and Tyson smiled at me. I could get used to that! Maybe we could be friends? It felt nice spending time with him when he was like this. But I was too naïve if I thought this time of serenity would last. I should've known something bad was about to happen.

We heard the front door opening with a bang, followed by an irritated and slightly slurred male voice.

"Damn car broke down two blocks away!" The voice was getting closer. "Better go fix it, boy, 'cause I'm gonna..."

The man stopped speaking when he entered the kitchen and saw me. He looked baffled for a second before a repulsive grin appeared on his face. He scanned my body with such a lustful glint in his bloodshot grey eyes that it made me want to smack him. Only then did I remember I was sitting there in nothing but a shirt and panties.

"Well, well, well..." He trailed off taking a few faltering steps. "What has my boy brought here? I don't like him having his whores in my house..." He got even closer and the stench of alcohol assaulted my nose. "But perhaps I should rethink that if they look like you, doll!"

"Stay away from her!" Tyson spat venomously at who I guessed was his father.

"My house, my rules, boy!" The man barked back at him but didn't take his eyes of my barely-covered legs.

I felt Tyson grab me by the arm and jerk me off of the counter. He quickly dragged me upstairs to his room, but before he could close the door we heard a voice shout from bellow:

"Use protection when you fuck her, boy! I'm not feeding another bastard!"

The boy shut the door with such force that it bounced off its frame and he had to close it again.

"Get dressed, Alex," he said with an emotion-drained voice.

"Tyson, I..." I started hesitantly, not really knowing what to say.

"I said get the fuck dressed damn it!" He bellowed and I let out a shriek, jumping up in the air. I quickly leaned down, took my jeans from the floor and put them on. I started to unbutton his shirt to replace it with my top but Tyson's voice cut me off.

"Leave it!" He demanded quietly and grabbed my wrist once again.

He hauled me out of his room, then out of the house and kept dragging me with him for a while. He finally stopped, pointing at a bench a few feet away.

"That's the bus stop," he announced coolly before leaving me on my own.

I guess being friends was out of the question now.

CHAPTER ELEVEN - Alex's past - PART ONE

T yson POV

Alex had just gotten on her ride. I left her by the buss stop but didn't stray far because I wanted to keep an eye on her. It wasn't smart for a girl to wander on her own in this neighborhood. Not even if she had Alex's skills.

Now that she was gone I needed to move. To where, I didn't know. It didn't really matter. I just didn't want to go back to the house. Not ever. But I knew I would have to return eventually. I couldn't afford to live on my own. Plus, I was still underage.

"Just a few more months!" I thought, counting down to my birthday. "Then I'll be free! I'll just have to try harder to avoid him till then."

Especially now. I wanted to kill him.

The way he looked at her... The way he talked to her... All that made me want to just pounce on that scumbag and hit him until he was unconscious. And then to hit him some more.

I sighed.

I needed to work. Right now. But I had to wait until it was evening. Then the Ring would provide me with the much desired arena to vend off my frustration. Tonight I wouldn't give a damn about the money; I just needed to fight!

But right now, I needed a smoke.

*****

The Ring rule number six: fights are one on one, two on two, one on two and, on special occasions, melees. The last provided the best way to unleash the beast within you which was exactly what I needed this evening. Unfortunately for me, tonight wasn't a special occasion. So I had to go with the second best choice: one on two. I would be fighting alone of course. As for my opponents... Well, I didn't really care who they were, as long as they were strong. It was for their own good to be so 'cause I was going all the way tonight.

No mercy for anyone!

*****

Alex POV

I was right - Tyson was fighting at the Ring tonight. I knew he would want... no, he would need to do so after what happened this morning. I would be doing the same if our roles were switched. At least I would want to... but he would never allow it. He never did. Although he knew he would make good money from me, not once did he even think to put me in the Ring. No. That would've attracted too much attention to me and I was too precious for him. I was his. At least he wanted it that way!

I sighed heavily. I was just starting to forget about him! And now here I was at the Ring – one of the places where he would make his money, so I could watch another guy fight.

I looked down at the arena just in time to see Tyson enter again. It was his third battle for the night; all of them were one on two with him fighting alone. He hadn't noticed me yet and I was hoping to keep it that way.

"Perhaps I should go home..." I thought. But I just couldn't keep my gaze away from the boy with the mismatched eyes.

The fight started.

God, he was beautiful!

And I didn't mean his face. The way he moved... It was pure poetry! It was hypnotizing! Fast, swift, accurate... So deadly in his fury! He was like a wild animal: lunging at his prey with both enough force and speed to cause maximum damage. He was out for blood tonight! He just couldn't get enough of it. Needless to say the battle was over quickly with one of his opponents too exhausted to get up and the other lying unconscious on the floor.

The sound of cheers erupted around me, mixed with the disappointed groans coming from those who no doubt had betted on the losers. Only then did I realize I was gaping in my amazement. That had been the third fight the boy won in a row.

Third and last because of Ring rule number seven: three matches at most per night unless on a special occasion. And special occasions indicated they were having some high rollers as VIP. Tonight wasn't such a night though.

Which meant it was time to go home. After all I'd come to the Ring with the sole purpose of watching Tyson. I didn't want to spend much time here; it brought too many memories.

*****

"I shouldn't have gone there!" I scolded myself, walking through the mostly empty streets. "I shouldn't have...But I wanted to see Tyson."

Only now that I was on my way back home from watching that boy fight at the Ring, I couldn't help the memories of him coming back.

The memories of Stefan.

It all started when we were children. Our families were friends, so naturally, we grew up together. Stefan had always been a stuck up, selfish rich brat but he had a soft and kind side for me... only for me.

He would be one of the three boys to always take care of me when I was little.

But when one of those boys died protecting me, little five-year-old me decided it was time to learn to take care of myself so I'll be the one protecting the important people in my life.

But my mother and father didn't think it was appropriate for their daughter to learn to fight. For years I had begged them to hire me a tutor who'd teach me the art of combat.

But they always refused me.

So who did I turn to? My childhood friend Stefan – a boy whose strict father was a big believer in violence because "fighting was the way to prove you are a real man".

I still had one more protector – my older cousin. But he lived in England so I rarely saw him. That left me alone with Stefan.

No wonder we got so close!

Only little me and little Stefan eventually grew up. And when that happened, we both changed. Because the now grown Stefan was in a gang and he was the alpha male there.

It started with him making a few new friends. He rolled with guys now but he kept me close by. We started going to parties, drinking and smoking weed (even I tried it a few times) and when we got bored of that, we would dare each other to play a prank on someone.

As time passed the challenges became more demanding and less than legal. The usual one was to steal something small from a person who pissed you or your pals off or to "borrow" a car; something I was particularly skillful at because I was good with vehicles.

Then somebody got the idea that instead of just "borrowing" cars and leaving them somewhere after a joy ride, we could steal them, sell them and enjoy spending the money. Most of the boys were upper-class and didn't need the extra cash; they just wanted to play gangsta.

And that's how Stefan's gang had started.

It consisted of roughly a dozen boys and me. Being the only girl, I had to constantly prove myself when challenged. It wasn't that hard for me; I was good at anything I was interested in. And if there was something new to be learned, I would be the first one to get the hang of it. But when they started with the illegal business, I wanted out. The only problem was that Stefan begged me to stay, convincing me I was the only one he could really trust.

So I stayed. I just couldn't leave my childhood friend on his own. Not after all he'd done for me.

But I never went with the boys on their raids.

The theft business was only one of Stefan's ways to make money. His father was a high roller at the Ring and he introduced it to his son, who introduced it to his gang in turn. Stefan sometimes fought himself but he would usually let his boys fight while he betted on them. He didn't let them take a dive; he said that would ruin the gang's image. But if they lost a fight in which he had betted on them, then they owed him money.

And Stefan was not the type of person you wanted to owe anything to.

The more he got involved in things like that, the more alienated he became from me. He knew that I disapproved so he tried to keep me away from it all because he didn't want to loose me.

But I knew. I always knew although I was foolishly hoping that he would change back to the way he was before.

But even though I did not steal cars or fight in the Ring, I found other ways to get in trouble. So one day my parents sent me off to England. They thought it was for the best; I wasn't the perfect little lady they wanted me to be so maybe a new environment would transform me into just that. But I got kicked out of school just a month after I arrived there so they had to take me back.

Imagine my surprise when Stefan came to pick me up from the airport. On his own. Without a single one of his boys. He said he missed me terribly; that he wasn't himself when I was away. He made me feel like when we were kids. I had such a good time catching up that we ended up spending the whole weekend together.

We slept together once. Then a second time. Eventually, we started dating.

And then he went back to his gang. At first it wasn't that bad. He would still be kind and attentive to me. But slowly he began treating me less as his girlfriend and equal and more as one of his subordinates.

Stefan's over-protectiveness had now turned into a sense of possession. He wanted me near even if all we did was fight. I was no longer a person; I was a trophy, evidence he could have anything he wanted. But I'd had enough. Enough of waiting and hoping that things will get better; enough of being captive.

So I left. I left him, I left the country.

And I came to the small town I'd called home for the past few weeks.

I sighed heavily.

Yep, I shouldn't have gone there. Thinking about Stefan always left me feel drained.

How did I not see sooner what he was like? Why didn't I leave earlier?

It wasn't only his possessiveness. He was now messing with drugs. No, he wasn't doing drugs; he was selling them. That had been the final straw! I just couldn't be around him anymore. Especially not after he knew my reason for hating them.

The man who killed my brother when I was five... He was on drugs. The man who was aiming at me... but shot him instead.

I was suffocating. I couldn't breathe. The familiar lump formed in my throat. But I knew I wouldn't cry. I'd lost that ability the day my brother was shot twelve years ago. I had not shed a single tear after that. Not even on his funeral.

I was almost at my apartment now. But I didn't go in. I needed to run.

So I turned on my heals and sped off in the opposite direction.

*****

I could feel it; the exhaustion taking over and replacing part of my sorrow. I knew the grief wouldn't go away completely; I knew it would come back to haunt me in my nightmares.

I was running through a park when I heard it: coughing. Not the I-have-a-cold type of cough but the I-can't-breathe one. I stopped and looked around, searching for the source of the noise.

My heart clenched at the sight of him.

Tyson was sitting on the ground, leaning his back on a bench and clutching his stomach. What had happened to him after the Ring? Instead of having just a few not too troublesome injuries, he was now covered in fresh bruises and cuts and was gasping for air.

"Tyson!" I ran to him.

"Alex?" He coughed out. "What... What are you... doing... here?"

"Tyson, what happened?" I ignored his question.

"I had... a little... dis... disagreement with..." He couldn't even finish one sentence; he was in that much pain. "... a pair... a pair of twins and... some friends of theirs."

Twins? His second battle tonight had been with twins. Maybe they decided to take revenge; it was not unheard of for people to do so after they got out of the Ring; that way there will be no rules whatsoever.

"Tyson, move your hands!"

Probably too tired to argue, he did as I told him. But instead of the stab wound I expected, I saw something else.

"Tyson, were you shot?"

"You just keep on... keep repeating my name tonight... don't you, Alex?" He smiled weakly at me. He wasn't paying attention to what I was saying and that was NOT a good sign. "I like that," he admitted quietly.

"Tyson, I need you to focus." I tried to keep my voice calm. "Were. You. Shot?"

"Don't... worry about it, Alex! It's not... really not serious. It just barely grazed my ribs... that's all."

"It still stings like a bitch," I remembered.

"How... would you know?" He asked, his mismatched eyes trying to focus on my face.

"Never mind. Can you get up?"

"I'm not sure."

"Damn it! Damn it... Damn it..."

*****

I had no choice; I brought Tyson to my apartment. The hospital was not an option 'cause they would ask too many questions. They would even get the police involved and that would cause some serious trouble for Ty: if he didn't speak to the officers, they'd arrest him; if he did talk to them and told them about the Ring... Let's say a prison stay will be heaven compared to what the people from the Ring would do to him!

My place was closer than the boy's house so naturally that's where I had headed. Besides, I was sure he wouldn't want to go to his house anyway. And I could keep an eye on him here.

I had finished taking care of his wounds. One more thing I learned thanks to my life with Stefan. He was never interested in mending wounds but he made sure I knew how to do that. One of the guys that worked for him taught me everything about patching up wounds ranging from an ordinary bruise, going through a small cut and finally - stab and gunshot wounds. The dude even showed me how to fix a dislocated shoulder or ankle. That is why we called him The Doctor, or Doc for short. He was the eldest in the gang, a guy in his twenties, and yet he hung out with us. I think being pressured by his parents to attend medical school, he never got to enjoy his teen years. So once he decided he had enough of being told what to do by mommy and daddy, he came to us. But enough about him!

I sighed, getting back to the present.

The good news was that Tyson had been right: the bullet had only slightly grazed him, it wasn't serious.

He was now sleeping in my bed. I myself was curled up on a bean bag in the same room. I wasn't eager to go to sleep; I knew the nightmares would come. Especially now that I saw a gunshot wound. It was just too close to home.

I knew that if I fell asleep now I would dream of my brother's death.

CHAPTER TWELVE - Alex's past - PART TWO

A /N: "Ne" means "No".

*****

Tyson POV

It was still dark when I woke up, with just enough light for me to realize I wasn't in my room. I looked around and noticing Alex's sleeping form it all came back to me: the Ring, the fight with the twins and a couple of their friends afterwards, the gun, how the girl found me in the park, brought me here to her place and tended to my wounds.

She wasn't kidding before when she said she was good at it!

Suddenly I heard her move and mutter something. I looked at her face and froze: she looked absolutely frantic.

"Ne." She raised her voice. "Ne, ne, ne!" Her voice was getting louder and louder and sounded more panicked by the second.

"Boris, ne! Ne! Ne! Ne! Ne! Boris! Ne!" She started screaming and trashing around, falling off the bean bag and on to the ground. But she still didn't wake up. "Boris! Boris! Ne! Ne!"

"Alex, open your eyes!" I shook her roughly. I couldn't even remember getting off the bed and coming to her side. Now I was the one loosing my nerve. "Alex! WAKE UP!"

"Ne, ne, Boris! Ne... NEEEE!" With one final shout she shot up to a sitting position and opened her eyes. Her gaze was distant as if she still wasn't in touch with reality.

"Alex..." I was surprised at how my voice sounded both worried and gentle at the same time.

"Tyson?" She turned to face me. She looked so... crushed.

Next thing I knew, I held her tightly in my arms, rocketing her gently back and forth, while running my hands soothingly over her back.

"Tyson..." She called tiredly after we had stayed like that for only God knows how long. "Tyson, you're injured. You should rest."

"I'm fine, Alex!" I didn't want to let her go; she seemed so fragile right now that if I did, she'd probably break.

"No, you're not! Go back to bed!"

"Only if you come with me."

"I'm fine here. I don't think I would be able to sleep anymore anyway..."

"Alex..."

"Tyson," she cut me off, "just go and rest. I'll be..."

But before Alex could finish, I lifted her up and carried her to bed, ignoring my body's painful protest. I knew I'd need to take it easy for quite a while in order to have my wounds heal properly, but I couldn't care less about that right now. I carefully placed the girl's small, shivering body on the bed then lay down next to her, hugging her close once more. She didn't try to break free from my grasp as I expected her to. Instead, she snuggled closer, wrapping her arms around me as well.

"Sweet dreams, Tyson!" She wished me quietly.

"Dreamless night, Alex!"

And I kissed her on the top of her head.

*****

Alex POV

I woke up securely wrapped in Tyson's arms. I felt so ashamed! I had let him see me at my weakest. It was hard enough to control the thoughts about my brother when I was awake, but it was completely impossible to do so when I was dreaming. It all came back full force then.

I sighed.

I shouldn't have fallen asleep! Especially not in the same room as Tyson. But I was worried about him and wanted to be around. And now he would despise me. I knew I did. I hated being so frail... so helpless whenever I thought about Boris.

I felt Tyson shift and turned to him just in time to see him opening his eyes. Two differently tinted orbs - one bright blue and one silvery-grey, both still filled with sleep, were looking at me, the emotions they held – unreadable.

"Hey!" The boy greeted softly... cautiously.

Oh, no! It was worse than I thought: he didn't despise me; he pitied me! I would choose him sneering at me any time over this!

"How are your wounds?" I queried, not wanting to talk about me.

"Much better. You're really good at this."

"Lots of practice," I announced rather coolly. I had decided I was going to pretend that last night didn't happen in hopes of him dropping the matter of my nightmares all together. "Do you want some breakfast?" I questioned getting off the bed.

"I wouldn't say no to some." He got up as well albeit slowly because of his injuries. He seemed to have picked up on my reluctance to talk because he was back to his usual distant demeanor.

"I'll go make us something. Why don't you take a shower in the mean time? I have some clean clothes you can borrow."

The boy started to laugh, but then immediately grimaced rubbing his ribs.

That must have hurt!

"I doubt anything you have will fit me, Alex."

"I still got your shirt." I had come home with it from his place.

"Keep it! It's too small for me now. Plus, it looks really good on you."

I didn't know why but I felt myself blush at his comment.

"Well, I could still lend you something. I have some boy clothes here as well."

His face darkened at my words. A humorless smile graced it.

"You want me to wear the clothes that guys you fucked forgot here? How many of those do you have exactly? Could they fill a wardrobe?" For some reason he sounded bitter.

"Actually, they are all Kevin's clothes. I bought them so he wouldn't have to carry too much luggage when he visits."

There was a glimmer of recognition in Tyson's eyes at Kevin's name. Have I mentioned him before?

"So, this guy Kevin..." He started slowly and gulped. What was with him today? "Is he... your boyfriend?"

"No!" I answered disgusted.

"'Cause you mentioned him before... When I woke you up at my place. You called me Kevin."

"That's because I used to live with him."

"You used to live with a guy?!" He sounded incredulous. "Alex, you're only seventeen!"

I burst out laughing at the face he made.

"Ty, Kevin is my cousin. He lives in London because his mother is from there, but he stays at my family's house when he comes to Bulgaria. And this apartment belongs to his father. My uncle doesn't use it anymore, but Kevin often visits... Mainly to check on me, if I have to be honest. So you can relax! You won't be wearing my ex's things. Actually, some of the clothes are brand new; my cousin hasn't even worn them yet. They won't be a perfect fit though 'cause he's a bit taller and bulkier than you."

"Oh!"

He seemed relieved at my words.

"Come on, let's get you something to wear!"

*****

Ty was still in the shower and I was making fried steak for breakfast. Yes, that classified as breakfast for me. Just as I took the last piece of meat out of the frying pan, I heard footsteps so I lifted my head.

Tyson came in dressed in light blue jeans and a black singlet. Still towel-drying his long damp hair, he looked at me puzzled.

"Steak? We're having fried steak for breakfast?"

"Even better: we're having steak sandwiches for breakfast!" I answered enthusiastically.

"Huh?"

"You'll see! But first: take off your clothes!"

"What?!"

"Take off your singlet; I have to take care of your wounds."

"Oh... That..."

He looked to the side in order to avoid my gaze, making me smirk; I knew what he must've thought about when I ordered him to take his clothes off.

"Where should I put this?" He waved the towel.

"Anywhere you like; I'll take care of it later."

Tyson sat himself down on a stool and placed the towel on another. He slowly took his singlet off, wincing slightly due to the pain. The majority of wounds were on his torso, but he had one on the left of his jaw, a split lip, as well as a black eye. I noticed the bruises had gotten a bluish hue during the night. I put on some ointment on them, aiming to be as gentle as possible, and then concentrated on the gunshot wound. I let out a relieved breath as it didn't seem to have gotten inflamed during the night.

The whole procedure of mending Tyson took about fifteen minutes. After that, I put away the medicine and focused on resuming making our breakfast.

"Ready to try out my steak sandwiches?" I asked, washing my hands.

"Okay…" He drawled, putting the borrowed singlet back on. The boy sounded more than a little suspicious of my cooking abilities. I had no idea why; I was a really good cook.

I began preparing our meal. I took out bread, mayo, potato chips and placed them on the counter. My sandwiches consisted of this: I'd take two slices of bread and put mayo on them. I'd smash the potato chips into little crumb-like pieces (sometimes I used cornflakes instead) and I'd place that on top of the mayo. I'd put a thin slice of steak on slice of bred number one and cover the whole thing with slice of bread number two and - Ta-da! – I'd have me a sandwich!

Tyson looked skeptically at my creation.

"Hey!" I exclaimed a little offended by the boy's evident lack of enthusiasm. "At least try it before giving me that face!" I passed him one of the sandwiches. He still looked unwilling to give it a go. "What's the matter, Ty?" I questioned him sweetly. "Do you want me to cut out the crusts for you?"

He snorted and took a single reluctant bite, which he chewed slowly. Then he took another - bigger one. Then another and another. In a minute the sandwich was all gone.

"Have any more of those?" He asked hopefully.

"Knew you'd like it!" I grinned, giving him one more and taking one for myself.

For a while we just munched on our food, keeping quiet. Unfortunately that gave me time to think about last night. My meal seemed to have lost its taste and I knew I was no longer smiling.

"Alex, what's wrong?" Concern was clear in the boy's voice.

"It was none of your business, Tyson!" I said firmly. "Just forget about what you saw last night, okay?"

He didn't answer and just stared at me with a blank expression. He absentmindedly chewed on his meal. Once the food was gone, he took a big gulp from the glass of water I'd placed before him. I watched him, noticing the thin lines that had formed on his forehead. The boy was obviously contemplating on something. But what?

"Alex..." He started in a quiet tone. "Who's Boris?"

I felt my eyes widen. Have I been talking in my sleep again? What did he hear? But I would usually speak Bulgarian... So even if Tyson had heard me, he wouldn't understand.

"He was my brother," I said in a low, even voice. I was surprised I'd answered; I rarely spoke about him with anyone but Kevin.

"Was?"

"He died when we were children."

Why was I still talking?

"I was about five and he wasn't even eight yet. We were at the store when an armed man came in. He pointed his gun at the cashier and demanded the money. He was so out of it, he didn't even see me standing there alone;

Boris was at the back of the store. The man behind the counter knew about me though. And his worried gaze fell on me. He didn't mean to give me away; it was an instinct, I guess. But the robber saw that and looked behind him. I must have startled him because he pointed the gun at me. All of a sudden Boris came up slowly from behind me, asking the man to lower his gun and telling him I was just a five year old girl; I couldn't hurt him. But what we didn't know at the time was that the guy was on drugs. He was shaking and he wasn't thinking clearly. So he fired a single shot at me..." I was surprised how steady my voice still was as I was confessing all this to Tyson. "The bullet grazed my left shoulder. I remember the pain that overtook me. But soon I no longer cared. Because I heard something heavy fall on the floor and when I turned around I saw it was Boris. The same bullet that sliced my skin went to his chest. He was still alive but barely breathing. He didn't make it. He was gone before the ambulance even came. I remember crying. And all I felt afterwards was emptiness. I can't even begin to describe how much we loved each other... how much we cared for each other. He was the most important person in my life. I haven't shed a single tear since that day. I learned to remember the good things about him; he wouldn't want me to be sad, I know that but... but sometimes at night... I just can't help it! When I dream of him dying again..." I laughed bitterly. "God, I'm pathetic!"

"You're not." The boy contradicted in a low voice.

"We both know I am, Tyson!" I snarled in irritation. "But I don't need your pity!"

"I don't pity you, Alex."

"Yeah, right!" I retorted, lowering my head; I couldn't even look at him.

"I'm serious, Alexandra!" He raised his voice. "All you've been through... and at such a young age... But you didn't let that bring you down. No. You used it to become stronger." He caught my chin between his thumb and forefinger lifting my head up. He captured my gaze with his and I could see the sincerity in those mismatched eyes. "Alex, you have no idea how much I admire you for that!"

I wanted to hug him. I wanted it so badly, to just embrace him like I did last night and to stay like that. I remembered the comfort it had brought me. But I didn't do it. I was done with my weak behavior. He'd seen too much already. So I settled for a nod and a small smile instead.

"Thank you! You know, you're nothing like…" I caught myself before I could finish.

"Nothing like who?" Tyson asked, tilting his head to the side and observing me with curiosity.

Should I answer him? He'd already heard some of my confessions… Why not go all the way? I didn't really want to share that with him, but something told me this boy wouldn't let it drop.

"Like Stefan," I sighed in defeat. "Back when we were kids Kevin used to live in Bulgaria so the four of us – him, me, Boris and Stefan, were always together. The boys used to take care of me because I was the only girl and the youngest in our little group. Well, Stefan is only a few months older but still… they were all very protective of me. But Boris died, Kevin moved to England and Stefan and I were left on our own. He was the one who thought me how to fight. But now he's… different." I had no desire to elaborate on that matter. "When I first met you, I thought you two were the same: cocky alfa males, both good fighters, both stuck up self-centered assholes… But I'm glad to say I was wrong about that; you might be alike but you're not the same. You should remember this moment, Ty; I'm very rarely mistaken." I heard him snicker at my comment. "Anyway, to make a long story short: Stefan and I aren't the best of pals now. I just couldn't take his attitude any more. Especially after I broke up with him…"

"You used to date the guy? I thought you said he was a prick?"

"I didn't use that word but it's a pretty accurate description." I laughed. "He wasn't always like that around me though so... yeah... we dated for a while."

"And then you dumped his sorry ass?"

"Yep. I dumped his sorry ass and came here to start anew. Away from him and his gang and away from trouble."

A crease formed on his forehead again.

"So that's why you were afraid to be seen fighting at school," he muttered. "Because fighting reminded you of him and the problems you used to have."

"Pretty much. Although, fighting you is just too tempting; I can't really help myself. You seem to be the only person around here to have that effect on me; to bring back bad girl Alex," I admitted a bit reluctantly.

Tyson fell silent once more. He looked thoughtful. After some time he slowly nodded. Whatever the boy had been contemplating on, he seemed to have finally reached some sort of decision.

"Thank you for the clothes and the breakfast, Alex," he said somehow estranged and got up. "I should get going."

"Oh...Yeah... sure!" I got up and I walked him to the door. I was confused by his sudden mood swing. What had caused it? Should I ask him that or let it go?

"Bye, Ty!"

He just nodded curtly and I closed the door behind him.

What had just happened? One minute he seemed attentive and empathetic and the next he was back to his old cold, not caring self.

Maybe that's what he was pondering about when he kept silent; if he really cared or not.

Obviously, he decided that he didn't.

I had finally opened up to someone and they didn't really care. Yes, I was pathetic! I should've just kept quiet about the whole thing. I'd always done that, so why had I felt the sudden urge to confide in someone? Why in Tyson? How was I to face him tomorrow at school?

I guess it was best to avoid the boy and pretend the last couple of days just didn't happen!

*****

Tyson POV

Too close to home.

Everything I represented was too close to home for Alex. Too painful. I had just reminded her of her dead brother and brought back her nightmares; I still somewhat reminded her of her ex; and I seem to be the only one to bring her back to her not so old habits by tempting her to fight me. And she'd come here to make a fresh start! That wouldn't happen if I was around her. So I made a decision: I would distance myself from the girl and let her be. Let her start anew and forget about her past.

Yes, I would avoid Alex the best I could; it was for her own good!

*****

A/N: I know that I've been writing some serious and dramatic chapters lately, but don't worry: next few will be humorous.

CHAPTER THIRTEEN
- Babies... Babies everywhere

A lex POV

It was the Monday after the whole embarrassing confession thing on my part. And after my decision to avoid Tyson like the plague.

The whole building was abuzz. Turns out another girl from our school got pregnant this year. At least this one was a senior, the first one being only a freshman. Apparently, the girl was dumb enough to share the news with her friends last Thursday. And of course by Monday everyone knew about it.

"Oh my God, Ally, did you hear?" Isabella squealed grabbing me by the arm. "One of the seniors got knocked up!"

I looked at her excited tanned face. I really thought Bella was a nice girl, but she was one of the biggest gossipers in our school. I mean, this blonde girl couldn't keep a secret if her damn life depended on it!

"Yes, Bells, I heard." I replied wearily. Her enthusiasm didn't falter at the obvious lack of enthusiasm in my response.

"I'm so going to tell the rest of the gang." And with that she left me.

"The chatty Bella cornered you too, huh?" Tara appeared to my left.

"Yep." I nodded. "Let's just get to homeroom!"

We greeted a few people on our way and chatted until we reached the room. Well, it was Tara who did most of the talking and I half-heartedly listened, letting out an "yeah" and an "aha" every now and then. My mind was still preoccupied by the events of the weekend.

We entered and I instinctively started searching for Tyson. I expected him to ditch today, but to my surprise, he was in his usual seat, gazing out the window. I briefly wondered why none of our classmates were staring at him; his black eye was hard to miss. But then I realized that they were probably used to seeing the boy in that state... And they had a much juicier gossip today.

The moment Tara and I had entered, we found our classmates in a state of animated gossiping about, you guessed it, the pregnant girl. Since she had yet to announce who the father was, some of the students were placing bets on it while others, a few boys actually, looked rather nervous. Could they be worried that the mystery man who impregnated the senior was one of them? Quite possibly; all the boys in question were players.

I was actually relieved when the teacher finally came in. At last! No more talk of unwanted teenage pregnancy and babies! But the topic didn't change even with Mr. Johnson in the classroom.

"Given the recent events," he started, "an emergency teachers-parents conference was held this Saturday morning. It was decided that you would be given these." He pointed at about a dozen boxes stacked atop of his desk.

"What are they?" One of our classmates asked.

"I was just getting to that!" Johnson responded testily. "They are Real Care Babies. For those of you who do not know what that is," he added when he saw the confusion on our faces, "I shall explain. Real Care Baby is a doll that makes it possible for people to practice caring for a baby. It's a 24/7 job. The doll makes realistic cries and you'll have to figure out what it needs: feeding, diaper changing, etc. Its software tracks if you are taking care of the baby and is it a safe handling. It records everything: exact times, missed care, specific mishandlings, head and neck support failure... It's the closest you'll get to the real thing. These babies will be given to all seniors as special project for a new Health class that you're going to be taking."

Here Tara raised her hand. Mr. Johnson nodded for her to speak.

"When will these extra Health classes be held?"

"Actually, we will be splitting Homeroom in two: you'll have twenty minutes of Homeroom and twenty of Health class. Anyway, you'll need to take good care of the babies because this whole thing will be graded." He was interrupted by a collective groan. "But wait! There is more!" He said swinging his hands dramatically in the air. "Since these things are expensive, the school decided that it will be better if you guys work in pairs so we could order less dolls..." Again he was interrupted by our raised voices.

"You won't be choosing your partners; you've already been paired on random." He shouted over us all.

When we finally calmed down, he started to read the list of who will partner with whom. Tara ended up with jock star Mike Barbson while I...

"Alexandra Atanasova, your baby daddy will be Tyson Williams."

*****

Tyson POV

"Alexandra Atanasova, your baby daddy will be Tyson Williams."

My head snapped up at the mention of my name. No! No, no, no, no, no! They can't pair me up with her. Anyone but her. Just yesterday I decided to keep away from her. Maybe I heard wrong. I turned to my right and saw the horrified look on Alex's face. Nope. I didn't hear wrong.

"You must be bloody joking..."

"You've got to be fucking kidding me..."

We both jumped from our seats, which wasn't smart on my part as the sudden movement made the gunshot wound sting. Ignoring the pain, I joined in on Alex's vigorous protest, but Mr. Johnson held up a hand to keep us quiet.

"I assure you both I'm completely serious. The list is final!" He added sternly when we begun to object again. "And no cursing in class or the two of you are getting detention! Well, the three of you now."

He handed Alex the doll and returned to his desk. The brunette stared dumbly at his back, disbelief etched on her face. I was pretty sure I looked the same.

"Tyson..." Her voice was so small I barely heard it. "Wh-what are we going to do?"

Her eyes were wide open and so was her mouth. Her gaze kept darting between me and the doll in her hands. She looked completely appalled.

"We're going to create a schedule and take care of the baby I guess..."

"But, Tyson, I don't know how to take care of babies!" She protested in a panicked voice.

"Do I look like I do?" I shot back.

"Bojichko, zashto az?!"

"What?"

"It means: "God, why me?"," the girl explained.

Wow. I guess the whole baby thing really freaked her out. I'd noticed she only spoke Bulgarian when she was angry, annoyed or upset. Or when she was cussing and didn't want the teachers to find out.

"Po dyavolite!"

"What?" I asked again.

"Damn it!" She translated. She closed her eyes and took a deep calming breath. She opened her chocolate browns and stared straight at my mismatched eyes, trying but failing to seem relaxed. "Okay! It can't be that bad, can it? I mean, you have some experience with Angel's siblings... right?" She added hopefully, begging me with her eyes to confirm that theory. The look she had was so desperate, I actually felt guilty that I couldn't.

"Nothing close to this," I responded, crushing all her hopes.

She groaned at my answer.

"Well, I guess we'll have to figure it out."

"Not like we have much of a choice!" I muttered.

*****

"Why should I get Fridays?" Alex asked furiously.

We were sitting on the ground, under a tree in the back courtyard, not far from the spot I took her to have our fight on her first Monday here. We were supposed to be discussing our schedule. Instead of that, we had been arguing for the last fifteen minutes and the both of us were running out of patience.

"Because I might be… busy then." I knew I had to take it easy for a while, but I'd eventually get back to the Ring. I didn't want to tell Alex I might be working on a Friday night, because then she would ask me what I was working as. And the less people who knew about what I did, the better.

"Oh, and I don't have social life?" She went on.

"Well, you'll just have to shag whoever you're screwing Friday night some other time! Maybe you could squeeze them in with your Saturday fuck-date."

"Does that mean you're watching it Saturday night?"

"No."

"And why not?" She asked through an exhale, trying to keep calm.

"Might be busy."

"Do you like pandas?" The girl queried out of the blue.

"Huh?" Was I could mutter, surprised by the random question.

"I asked if you liked pandas. Because if you keep replying with "might be busy", I'll turn you into one!"

I rolled my eyes at her threat to smack me and give me another black eye.

"Now back to the schedule," she went on. "Friday or Saturday? Which do you choose?"

"Neither."

"Tyson Williams, you're not getting the whole damn weekend off!" She screamed at me just as "our baby" started crying again. "Oh, shut the fuck up or I'm going to leave you in front of some church!" She shouted at it.

"I pity your future kids if this is how you handle children," I stated, taking the doll and rocking it gently.

"It's just some damn doll. Besides, the moment I get pregnant, I'm getting an abortion. I don't want any kids; not now, not ever!" She seemed completely serious about it.

"You seemed pretty comfortable with Angel's siblings," I mentioned, remembering the time we babysitted together.

"Well, they are pretty cool kids. And they are past the baby stage," she added, glaring at the doll I was still swaying. A moment later, it stopped crying and fell asleep.

"You see that; you know how to take care of it." She said. Then her face suddenly lit up as she thought of something. I really didn't like the way she was looking and grinning at me now; I was sure I wasn't going to enjoy whatever brilliant idea she had just come up with. "Hey, how about I pay you to look after it all the time? Kind of like being a single parent who gets child support."

At first I gapped at her, shocked by what she had just proposed. How the fuck was I supposed to take care of the doll on my own, all the time?

"You better be joking!"

"Oh, come on, Ty!" She whined. "I don't even know how to hold the damn thing let alone fucking take care of it."

I sighed heavily and put the baby down.

"You pick it up like this…" I got the doll in my arms again, "and hold it like this. You can do it; I've seen you holding that cat that hangs around the school in this very position. It's the same thing, only with a person instead of an animal."

"You mean a doll instead of an animal." She rolled her eyes at me. "I wish they'd given us kittens or puppies instead. Animals are cute and human babies are plain ugly."

"Alex, let's just get back to the schedule!" I pleaded tiredly.

"How about this: I get Mondays, Wednesdays and Fridays and you get Tuesdays, Thursdays and Saturdays. This week I get Sunday, next week you get that day and so on and so on until we're done with this torturous project?"

"Seem fair," I uttered cautiously, searching for the catch. There had to be one; Alex was not to be relied on about this, she really wanted nothing to do with that doll. And yet I couldn't find any signs of deception. Maybe she had just given up and decided that in the end honesty was the best policy.

"Fine! Now give me the bloody thing," the girl commanded, getting up and placing her rucksack on her back. "I gotta go!"

I handed her the baby. The moment she touched the doll, it started crying.

*****

A/N: Alex has her reasons to act that way around babies and you can read about them later on.